Matias was such a good actor, Georgina thought. The warm voice, the light touches, the easy proximity...

He was probably thinking of the next big deal he had to complete while playing the attentive lover, but no one would ever have guessed, least of all his mother, who looked as though Christmas had come early.

She gathered herself and smiled brightly. "Of course...*darling*..." Busying herself pouring another cup of tea killed a couple of minutes, during which time Matias sauntered toward the kitchen table, where she had sat back down, and rested his hands lightly on her shoulders.

He gently massaged the nape of her neck then lifted her hair to feather a kiss where his massaging thumbs had been.

Breathing became difficult. This was totally out of order, she thought furiously. Some semblance of affection might be passable but *this*...?

"What," he murmured, thankfully straightening although keeping his hands on her shoulders, "was it that made you fall head over heels in love with me?"

Cathy Williams can remember reading Harlequin books as a teenager, and now that she is writing them, she remains an avid fan. For her, there is nothing like creating romantic stories and engaging plots, and each and every book is a new adventure. Cathy lives in London, and her three daughters—Charlotte, Olivia and Emma—have always been, and continue to be, the greatest inspirations in her life.

Books by Cathy Williams

Harlequin Presents

The Secret Sanchez Heir
Bought to Wear the Billionaire's Ring
Cipriani's Innocent Captive
Legacy of His Revenge
A Deal for Her Innocence
A Diamond Deal with Her Boss
The Tycoon's Ultimate Conquest
Contracted for the Spaniard's Heir

One Night With Consequences

Bound by the Billionaire's Baby
The Italian's One-Night Consequence

Visit the Author Profile page
at Harlequin.com for more titles.

Cathy Williams

MARRIAGE BARGAIN WITH HIS INNOCENT

HARLEQUIN PRESENTS®

Recycling programs
for this product may
not exist in your area.

ISBN-13: 978-1-335-47831-3

Marriage Bargain with His Innocent

First North American publication 2019

Copyright © 2019 by Cathy Williams

Printed in U.S.A.

MARRIAGE BARGAIN
WITH HIS INNOCENT

CHAPTER ONE

GEORGINA LOOKED UP at the imposing Georgian mansion in front of which she was standing. Well, she would have expected nothing less.

She raised her hand to the doorbell. Her brain was saying *Might as well get it over and done with* while her feet were yelling *Hang on just a minute... let's think about this.*

She went with the brain and pressed the buzzer before her feet could start winning the argument.

She was here now. She'd travelled hours to be here and she wasn't going to slink away without telling the owner of this over-the-top mansion in Kensington—a man she had known since childhood, a man on whom she had had a very inconvenient crush when she'd been a kid of sixteen, —that, *Hey...guess what...? I bet you never thought that you and I would be in a relationship after all!*

Matias had no idea who could be ringing his doorbell, but whoever it was deserved a Medal of Honour for the most timely interruption in history.

The icy blonde perched on his white leather sofa hadn't stopped screaming for the past thirty-five minutes. She carried on screaming now, as she followed him out of the vast sitting room towards the front door.

'I refuse to let you break up with me! I've told *everyone* that you'll be coming to the anniversary party next weekend! I've bought a *dress*! There's someone else, isn't there? Who is she? Do I know her? How could you *do* this to me? I love you! I thought you loved *me*!'

Matias had stopped answering her questions ten minutes ago and he wasn't going to start again now.

He pulled open the door and stopped short.

'Matias.' Georgina peered around him to the source of the high-pitched screaming. 'I'm guessing I've come at a bad time?'

The feet were desperate to take to the hills, but she wasn't quitting now that she was here. That said, she wanted to do nothing more than run away, because it didn't matter how much she braced herself for Matias's ridiculously stupendous good looks, every single time she saw him she was floored all over again.

Dry mouth, thudding heart, clogged brain…and a crashing reminder of what it had felt like to be an adolescent, with her hormones wildly out of control, in thrall to a guy who had never been short of his own personal fan club full of adoring hot babes from the age of thirteen. She'd kept her idiotic crush under wraps, but she could still burn with shame at the memory of it because she'd always been the last sort of girl he would ever have looked at.

'Georgie, what the hell are you doing here?'

'That's not a very nice way to greet an old friend, is it? I'd rather not come back, Matias. I've spent hours on a train and I'm hot and tired and my feet need to rest.' *Or to take flight*, she thought, willing her nerves to go away and thinking, yet again, how much she disliked the man. So stupidly sexy, and yet with a set of values that *so* got on her nerves.

'Is my mother all right?' Matias demanded.

'Who are *you*?'

A blonde had materialised next to him and Georgina wondered whether Matias ever got bored of dating women who were clones of one another. Towering blondes with catwalk figures and a racy sense of fashion that was based on wearing as little as possible even in the depths of winter.

This particular blonde was wearing a tiny red mini-skirt and a tiny red top and some very high sandals because it was the height of summer.

'Time for you to go, Ava.'

'We could still make this work, Matias!'

Matias cast a sideways look at Georgina and raked his fingers through his hair. 'No chance,' he said grimly, rescuing her tiny tan designer bag from the table in the hall and handing it to her while channelling her towards the doorway. 'You deserve better than me.'

Georgina rolled her eyes. She stood aside while

the blonde walked past her, at least eight inches taller in her heels and as skinny as a runner bean.

'That was considerate of you, Matias—softening the blow by telling her that she could do better than you,' Georgina remarked, stepping inside the mansion and getting a glimpse of his departing back as he headed towards some other part of the house—probably the kitchen, because he looked as if he could use a stiff drink.

Charming, she thought, walking briskly behind him. What on earth did all those women see in him? Yes, he was rich. Yes, he was good-looking. But beyond that... There was nothing that appealed on any level. Which made it quite ironic, considering she was here to tell him that they had secretly been seeing one another, falling in love and getting embroiled in a hot and heavy relationship that was destined to lead...*who knew where?*

She felt queasy at the revelations about to be put on the table.

'Well?'

Matias didn't bother looking at her. He went straight to a cupboard, pulled out a bottle of whisky and poured himself a glass, offering her one as an afterthought, but obviously not really expecting her to take him up on the offer.

'Your mother is fine. In a manner of speaking.'

'I've had a hellish day, Georgie, so spare me the riddles. Not that it's like you to beat about the bush. Bludgeon it into the ground is far more your style.'

He raised his eyebrows and didn't look away when their eyes tangled. 'I spoke to my mother two days ago and she sounded well, so what's the matter with her?'

'Nothing. Her health hasn't deteriorated. I mean, she's still weak after the stroke, and her speech isn't quite back to normal, but she's doing all the exercises the doctor recommended.'

'Good.'

'You have a wonderful house, Matias.' She didn't feel that the subject waiting to be broached could be broached quite yet. She needed to feel a bit more comfortable. Right now, her nerves were at breaking point. 'And I *will* have that drink you offered, actually.'

'Whisky?'

'Wine, if you have any. Thank you.'

'I'm warning you it's not organic. It's incredibly expensive, though, so please think twice about pouring it down the sink because it fails to meet your high standards.'

Matias strolled towards the fridge and withdrew a bottle of Chablis. He looked at her over his shoulder. She was dressed as she was always dressed, in some sort of flowery concoction that was designed to do absolutely nothing whatsoever for the female form. Long skirt, loose top... A veritable riot of colours, none of which flattered a woman who was small, round and had bright red hair.

Was it *so* hard to make an effort? he wondered.

'Very funny, Matias.'

'We both know how much you like to bang the drum for organic farming. I wouldn't want to get in the way of your social conscience.'

'You can be really horrible, do you know that?' she asked. But her voice was neutral, because she was busy looking round the spectacular kitchen with its shiny gadgets and space-age feel.

'You'd miss it if I wasn't,' Matias murmured without batting an eye, and he held her gaze for a few seconds longer than strictly necessary before lowering his eyes, letting his lush dark lashes shield his expression. 'What would you do with a nice, *polite* Matias?'

Georgina blushed—much to her annoyance—and glared. 'I've spent hours travelling here to see you. The least you could do is to be nice to me.'

'Yes, you have,' Matias said thoughtfully, 'and I'm wondering why. In fact, I'd go so far as to say I'm burning up with curiosity. I don't think you've ever come to this house, have you?'

'You know I haven't.'

'In fact, I didn't think you ever got out of deepest, darkest Cornwall.'

'You've always been so scathing about Cornwall! Don't you have *any* loyalty to the place where you were brought up?'

'No. So, moving on, Georgie…' He circled her the way a shark might circle a minnow, slowly, thoroughly, and with keen, watchful interest. 'If you're not here to talk about my mother, then what exactly *are* you doing here? Not that your arrival wasn't opportune.'

He sat on the chair facing her and tugged another chair towards him so that he could stretch out his long legs.

Georgina opened her voice to give him a piece of her mind. His mother despaired of him. His women came and went with barely a pause for breath in between, because Matias Silva had the attention span of a toddler in a candy shop when it came to women.

She caught the veiled amused expression in his dark eyes and abruptly shut her mouth. He wanted to get a rise out of her and that was the last thing she needed.

Instead, she met his gaze steadily and coolly. It took willpower, because he was, without doubt, the most drop-dead gorgeous man she had ever seen. Blessed with the exotic genes of his Argentinian father and the spectacular beauty of his English mother, Matias had emerged into the world with the sort of physical advantages that made people stare and then turn around for a second look, because surely no one could be quite so spectacular.

She had long ago forgiven herself for her girlish crush. She just wished that her disobedient eyes could stop drinking him in the way they were doing right now.

His features were chiselled to perfection, but his bronzed colouring and raven-dark hair, which he always kept slightly too long, rescued him from being just another good-looking guy.

'I *am* here to talk to you about your mother,' Georgina said into the lengthening silence. 'But could I just unwind for a bit? I'm exhausted.'

'It's seven o'clock. Have you eaten?'

'I had some sandwiches on the train.'

'I'll take you out to dinner.'

'I doubt I'm dressed for the sort of restaurants *you're* likely to patronise,' Georgina said wryly.

'How would you know what sort of restaurants I'd be likely to patronise?' he asked.

But he was smiling crookedly at her, reminding her that beneath their obvious, glaring and insurmountable differences, there were times when they were eerily tuned in to one another. Longevity and history, she presumed.

'Because I'm smart like that.' She was beginning to feel overheated. 'Thank you. It's very nice of you. But…er…no, thank you. Why don't you show me round your lovely house? I'd far rather that.'

The plan Georgina had sketched out had been a hurried one—a response to circumstances, formulated on impulse and put on the table before she'd had time to think through the details and, more to the point, the glaring, inescapable downsides. By the time she'd sat back and thought about it, it had been too late to take it all back.

Rose Silva believed that her son was finally on the verge of settling down, if not with the girl of *his* dreams, then certainly the girl of *hers*. She adored Georgina.

She finally had something to live for. She would have a daughter-in-law she loved. Her son would be settled, as he should be, with no more of his silly cavorting with women who weren't suited to him at all. There would be grandchildren. All would be right in the world.

In the space of five minutes, Georgie's suggestion of a relationship with Matias had turned into a full-blown *when-shall-I-start-looking-for-a-hat?* response. Georgie had squashed that enormous leap as firmly as she could, but here she was, supposedly having a serious relationship with the guy looking at her now with those fabulous dark, dark eyes.

What had begun as an ill-thought-out but well-intentioned little white lie had taken on a life of its own faster than a rocket soaring into space. An entire future had been planned before Georgina had had time to draw breath—and now here she was.

'Please don't say a word to Matias,' she had begged Rose, horrified at the thought of a congratulatory phone call to a guy who would have no idea what his mother was going on about. 'We…er… planned on breaking it to you together… Just that we're going out, Rose… Who knows where that will lead…?'

The feeble utterances had actually brought her out in a cold sweat and prompted her immediate departure to London. As his newly acquired girlfriend, didn't she need to know the layout of his house? She still felt queasy.

'You want to see my house? Why?'

'You're so scornful whenever you come down to Cornwall… I want to see what you have here that's so superior.'

Matias tilted his head to one side and looked at her carefully. 'Why am I getting the feeling that something's going on here that I don't know about?'

'You don't have to show me around if you don't want to.'

'Bring your drink. Maybe after a bit of alcohol you'll tell me exactly what's going on, Georgie.'

'Why are you so suspicious?'

'Because I wasn't born yesterday. I also *know* you. Some might say better than I've ever known any woman. You're here for a reason, and if it's not because my mother needs me to come down to Cornwall for health reasons, then you're here for something else and you're too scared to come right out and tell me. Is it money?'

On his way to the sitting room to begin the grand tour, Matias stopped abruptly and looked at Georgina through narrowed eyes. He positioned himself so close to her that she could pick up the faint whiff of whatever expensive aftershave he wore. She automatically edged back.

'You think I'm here to…to ask you for *money*? And you claim to *know* me?'

'It's not that far-fetched.' Matias shrugged. 'You'd

be surprised how many people come crawling out of the woodwork to ask for money when they find out that I'm in a position to bestow it upon them.'

'Why would I have to ask you for *money*, Matias? I have a job! I'm a food photographer! By your lofty standards it may not pay much, but it's more than enough for me to live on! So why on earth would I have to come to you for a loan?'

'No idea. Who knows what sort of financial trouble you might have got yourself into?'

He spun round and Georgina stared at him with outrage. No one had ever been able to rile her as much as Matias Silva. Or challenge her. Or generally send her nervous system into frantic overdrive. He was right. They *knew* one another—whether she cared to admit it or not.

From the side-lines she had watched the way he had turned into a forbidding and coolly remote adolescent after he had won a scholarship to a boarding school in Winchester. All pretence of having any interest in his parents' organic farm had been dumped. Ambition had become his constant companion.

It was little wonder that he was now wondering whether she had shown up on his doorstep out of the blue because she needed a hand-out. For Matias, money was the only thing that made any sense. He'd never had much growing up, and he'd made it his life's work to compensate for the lack.

Was it any wonder that they rubbed one another up the wrong way when they were as different as chalk and cheese? She was argumentative. He was intransigent. She was uninterested in money. Money was all he cared about. She loved where she lived. He hadn't been able to wait to escape from it. She admired his parents. He privately scorned them.

'Well? Spit it out, Georgie. Do you need a loan?'

He looked her up and down, head inclined to one side, his dark eyes coolly speculative. She didn't think there was a man alive who got on her nerves more.

'Have you been living beyond your means?' he murmured with exaggerated interest. 'Nothing to be ashamed of. Oh, wait... I can see why you *might* be ashamed, bearing in mind your holier-than-thou outlook on life which you've spent the past ten years droning on about.'

Georgina gritted her teeth and balled her hands into fists. 'I'm not here to ask you for money, Matias.'

'Didn't think you were.' He moved off to begin their tour, pushing open doors without bothering to explain which room was used for what.

'Why's that?' she asked.

All white. Minimalist. Big, expensive abstract art on the walls. A lot of chrome. The best money could buy. Again, no surprise there. Matias had gone to university a year early, studied Maths and Economics, and left with a job at an investment bank in his hand. Within five years he had made his first million and then he had started flying solo, buying up sick companies and turning them around. He'd invested in property on the side. By thirty he'd had an empire under his belt and more money than anyone could use in a lifetime. Every room she glimpsed bore witness to how rich he was.

No wonder Rose was intimidated by her billionaire only child.

'He's always been something of a genius,' she'd once confided wistfully. 'That's why he's never liked the simple life. It isn't enough for him.'

'Georgie,' Matias was saying now, 'it doesn't take a genius, looking at you, to realise that you have *no* interest in *anything* that could possibly get someone into debt.'

'What's that supposed to mean?'

'You're not the typical picture of someone leading a raunchy life beyond her means. If you have a predilection for designer clothes, fast cars and jewellery then you're doing a damn good job of keeping it under wraps. Besides…I remember you showing me your piggy bank when you a kid. You were very proud of the eight pounds sixty you'd managed to stockpile over six weeks. It would beggar belief that you'd go from parsimonious and proud saver to wildly extravagant spender. Now, do you want the tour to carry on upstairs?'

He looked at her and she wondered whether he realised just how offensive he could be.

'Or have you relaxed sufficiently to tell me why you're here? You may have had sandwiches on the train, but I'm hungry. I'll get some food delivered.

Let me know if you want to see the rest of the house and I'll order when the tour is done.'

'No—no need to go upstairs.'

She thought *bedrooms* and backed away from the thought fast. Despite loathing the man, it had always been way too easy to associate him with bedrooms— partly because he was so sexy, and partly because, even though time had moved on from that girlish in- fatuation, age had failed to completely extinguish the remnants of her crush. She still occasionally caught herself daydreaming about him. Fortunately she'd learnt how to avoid getting too embroiled in that kind of pointless fantasy.

'Good.' He headed back towards the kitchen, phoning for food on the way. 'Where were you plan- ning on spending the night?'

He looked at the battered khaki backpack which she had dumped on the ground in the kitchen.

'B&B.'

Matias frowned. 'That's ridiculous,' he said shortly. 'Didn't you consider staying here? Don't you think I'm not appreciative for everything you do for my mother and have done over the years? A night in my house is the least I could offer in re- turn.'

Georgina flushed. 'I shouldn't be the one doing stuff for your mother, though, should I?' she mut- tered, fidgeting.

'When it comes to that old chestnut—been there, done that. I've heard every variation of criticism from you over the years, so let's drop the topic and move on.'

Matias felt a flash of guilt dart through him like quicksilver. He had no reason to feel guilty. None at all. He supported his mother financially, made sure she wanted for nothing. It took hard work to make the sort of money that he did, and without his money life would not be nearly so rosy for his mother. When things went wrong in her house he made sure to replace them with top-of-the-range equivalents. Over time, her kitchen had been so expensively kitted out that any professional chef would have been happy to ply his trade there. And as for the farm...

The organic farm she'd insisted on hanging on to brought in peanuts and she couldn't have begun to handle it without his help. He made sure that everyone who worked there reported to him—just as he made sure that any headaches were sorted before they became full-blown.

And organic farming—as he had discovered years ago—was nothing but one long, grinding headache. Crops had a nasty habit of falling victim to the wrong type of insect. The chickens, which had made a brief and optimistic appearance for a year and a half, had fallen prey to foxes or else wandered off hither and thither to lay eggs that couldn't be located and therefore never made it to the shelves at the local greengrocer.

Although, in fairness, it was better than the Reiki treatment, the donkey sanctuary, the creative workshops and the gem-selling crackpot ideas that had preceded the farm when he'd been a kid.

So guilt? No, he had nothing to feel guilty about. He and his mother might not be close, but how many relationships between children and their parents were trouble-free? He was a responsible and dutiful son, and if his mother thought that he came up short in the personal stakes then he could live with that.

He shook his head free of inconvenient introspection and surfaced to find Georgie apologising.

'Sorry?' His eyebrows shot up. 'You're *sorry* about criticising?' He grinned. 'Now I'm *really* getting worried. Since when have you ever made apologies for getting under my skin?'

He watched as she noticeably didn't answer but instead devoted her attention to inspecting the rooms they had previously walked past.

Just when he was about to break the ever-lengthening silence the doorbell went. When Matias returned, it was with a spread of food from a top London restaurant.

'I've ordered enough for two,' he said, dumping the lot on the table and hunting down two plates and some cutlery. He poured them both wine and sat facing her.

'Most people have Indian or Chinese take-out,' Georgina remarked.

She shouldn't eat. She had had those sandwiches and she could do with shedding a few pounds. But her mouth watered at the sight of fluffy white rice, beef in wine, vegetables...

'Dig in,' Matias encouraged drily. 'But save room for the chocolate fondant.'

'My favourite.'

'I know. I recall going to that restaurant by the sea years ago, with my parents and your family, and you made them bring you three. Eat—and tell me exactly what you're doing here. I'm bored with going round the houses.'

'It's about your mother, but not about her health as such. Like I said, she's doing as well as can be expected, and I know you've paid for the best consultants, the best hospital, the best of everything... But health isn't just a physical thing. It's also a frame of mind, and your mum's been depressed for quite a while.'

'Depressed?' Matias frowned. 'Why would she be depressed when she's on the mend? She didn't sound depressed when I spoke to her last.'

'She wouldn't have wanted to worry you, Matias,' Georgina said impatiently. 'She's been making noises about her mortality. She's waiting for some test results—perhaps that's been preying on her mind—but she could be in a mental slump.'

'Test results? What test results? At any rate, they can't be important or the consultant would have mentioned them to me. And thoughts of her mortality? She's not even in her mid-sixties!'

He relaxed. If this was a simple case of hypochondria then an informal chat with her consultant would soon make her see sense. She was on the road to recovery. Mortality thoughts were only appropriate for people in their eighties and nineties, anyway.

He had a couple of big deals on the go, but as soon as he was through with those he would go down to Cornwall. He might even consider staying longer than a weekend. It could work... He had had the fastest possible broadband installed in his mother's house years previously, because he couldn't function without the Internet. In short, he could spare a little time down there without it affecting his work schedule.

'She's got another thirty years in her,' he said, noting that for someone who had refused the offer of a meal out Georgie had certainly done justice to the food on her plate. No one could ever accuse Georgina White of having a feeble appetite. It was a refreshing change, in actual fact.

'She doesn't see it that way.'

'*She* doesn't have a medical background. The consultant has no worries about her health or I would know about it. That's what he's paid to do—keep me in the loop. It's just a question of convincing her of that. If she's concerned that there's a risk of this thing happening again, then I can get Chivers to show her the charts and scans.'

'It's not just a question of that, Matias. She feels...' Georgina sighed and gazed at him, then wished she hadn't because she couldn't seem to tear her eyes away. He was so ridiculously good-looking. 'She feels that she's been a failure as a mother. She feels that there's a chasm between you two and it's one that will never be breached. All she wants, she tells me, is for you to settle down…have a wife and kids. She tells me that she's always wanted to be a grandmother and that she feels there's nothing to look forward to. When I say that she's depressed, it isn't because she thinks she might be pushing up the daisies in six months' time. It's because she's been looking back on her past and questioning where she is right now—in the present. I've had a word with Mr Chivers… I hope you don't mind.'

'It wouldn't make any difference if I said I did, would it? Considering you've already contacted him.'

Matias scowled. The guilt was back and with a vengeance. It seemed it had been buried in a very shallow grave. His mother had never been impressed with his lifestyle or his money. Nor had his father, when he had been alive. Neither had ever said anything, but their silence on the subject had spoken volumes.

'What did he say?'

'He says that under normal circumstances he wouldn't be worried. Rose is young. But because of her anxieties, and the subsequent stress, there's a chance that her health might be jeopardised. She's lost interest in all the things that used to occupy her. She doesn't seem to care about the farm any more.

She's not going to the gardening club. Like I said, she's talking about having nothing to live for.'

'You could have just called to fill me in on all this. Leave it with me. I'll have a word with Chivers. I'm paying the man a small fortune. He should be able to do *something*. There might be a course of medication my mother could go on…there are tablets for that sort of thing.'

'Forget it. It won't work,' Georgina told him bluntly.

Matias frowned, his brooding dark eyes betraying the puzzlement of someone trying to join dots that weren't quite forming a pattern.

'Then what will?' he asked, with an elaborate show of patience that got on her nerves.

'You'll probably need something stiffer than a glass of expensive white wine before I tell you my solution.'

'Spit it out. I can't bear the suspense.'

'I may have told her a couple of tiny white lies…' Georgina stuck out her chin at a pugnacious angle— an angle that said that she was a woman about to dig her heels in and was ready for a fight if he wanted to have one.

Now that they were getting to the heart of the matter, her nerves were kicking in big time.

'You *may* have told her a couple of tiny white lies…? Now, why does that admission send a shiver of apprehension racing down my spine?'

'I love your mother. I've always been close to her,

as you well know, and more especially now, since my parents decamped to Melbourne for my dad's three-year secondment to the university there. I've been with her throughout this awful business, and you can trust me when I tell you that her spirits are sinking lower and lower by the day. Who knows what could happen?'

'Yes, I'm getting the picture. You've known my mother since the dawn of time and you're worried about her, despite hard evidence from the experts that everything's ticking along nicely. So, Georgie, just say what you have to say—because my apprehension is still there. Why don't we dump this meandering, getting-nowhere-fast route and stick to the main road? In fact, why don't we just return to those little white lies of yours?'

'Okay, Matias… I *may* have encouraged your mother to feel that she has every right to look forward to the future…'

'Bracing advice.'

'Because you're involved with someone, and happily it's not one of those women your mother disapproves of.'

'The more I hear, the more I ask myself whether you and my mother have any topic of conversation aside from me.'

'We *never* talk about you!' Georgina snapped, momentarily distracted by the sheer egotism of the man. 'It's only because of the situation that she's taken to confiding in me… Naturally I'm not going

to tell her to keep her worries and fears to herself…
Trust me when I tell you that I *don't* encourage her
to talk about you!'

'Let's leave that to one side for the while. So, I'm
involved with someone my mother approves of? I
suppose, as fairy stories go, that one could work—
provided I'm not called upon to introduce this para-
gon to her. Because if I am, then it's going to take
a lot more than creative spin to cover up the cracks
in your plan.'

'Well, you see, this is where it may be less difficult than you imagine…'

She cleared her throat. She couldn't carry on—
especially when he was staring at her narrowly, his
clever brain whirring away to make sense of what
she'd just said. She inhaled deeply and reminded
herself that this was why she was here—this was
why she had made this inconvenient trip to London
to see a man who had always managed to rub her
up the wrong way.

She was here to do a *job*, so to speak.

Yes, she had acted on impulse—but impulse was
not a dangerous thing because it was a *good* thing.
All she had to do was look ahead to the good that
could come out of it. And not be deterred by those
bitter-chocolate-dark eyes staring at her with off-
putting intensity.

'I'm all ears.'

'I've told your mother that you and I are an item,'
she said in a challenging voice.

It came out in a rush and left behind a silence that was thick and dense and so uncomfortable that she could only stare down at her sandals while wishing that the ground would open up and swallow her whole.

Oh, how different the whole thing had seemed when she had told Rose. She had watched how the older woman's thin face had lit up. Rose had actually clapped her hands with delight, and Georgina had had a wonderful moment of basking in the warm glow of having made someone she loved very happy.

Before common sense had set in. By which time it had been too late to retract what she had said and the warm glow had been replaced by an icy, clammy dread.

Right now, right here, she wondered what had possessed her. How on earth could she have thought that this might be a good idea? She had travelled up to London prepared to stand her ground and fight her corner, but she had forgotten how intimidating Matias could be.

Why had impulse galloped ahead of common sense?

'Sorry?' Matias inclined his head with an expression of rampant disbelief. 'I think I may have misheard what you just said…'

CHAPTER TWO

'YOU HAVEN'T,' GEORGINA said flatly.

'Okay. So let me run this past you and you can tell me if I've got anything wrong. My mother is feeling a bit low…'

'With all the signs of depression…'

'Which could probably be taken care of with a course of tablets, because—believe it or not—tablets *do* exist for conditions like depression. But you've unilaterally, and without bothering to consult me, decided to rule that practical solution out.'

'You're making it sound so black and white and it's not. Which is something you would see if you were around a little more often!'

'Let's leave the criticisms to one side for the time being, Georgie. In a nutshell, my mother is down, wishes she could hear the pitter-patter of tiny feet, and to oblige her and raise her spirits you've decided to tell her a whopper about you and I being involved.'

'You should have seen the expression on her face, Matias. She hasn't looked so overjoyed in… Well, I would say *years*. Not since your dad died. Even before the stroke!'

Matias looked anything but overjoyed. His expression was a mixture of outraged incredulity and simmering anger. Of course she hadn't expected immediate capitulation, because that would have been too good to be true, but she saw she was going to have to use all her powers of persuasion. She couldn't bear the thought of his mother fading away into a chronic depression.

Even after Antonio's death Rose hadn't sunk into the sort of dull-eyed, low-level despair Georgina had begun to notice in her recently. The fact that tests were still ongoing was simply feeding into her acceptance that the road she was travelling was heading sharply downwards. She was ill, she was down, and nothing was ever going to change.

Until now Georgie hadn't really appreciated just how much of a surrogate mother Rose had become for her. Her own mother, whom she loved dearly, was worlds apart from her, wrapped up in academia—a world with which Georgina was unfamiliar. She had never got her intellect going, never been able to follow in her parents' intellectual footsteps. Her father lectured in economics, her mother in international law.

She, on the other hand, even from a young age, had been a lot happier being creative. It was to her parents' credit that they had never tried to push her towards a career she would have had no hope of achieving, and while they had busied themselves with university stuff Georgina, growing up, had drifted off to Matias's house, bonded with his parents and adored their wacky creativity.

She *loved* his mother, and that thought put a bit of much-needed steel in her weakening resolve.

'If I didn't know better,' Matias said, 'I would be inclined to think that you've finally cracked. And here's a little question, Georgie—*why* would my mother believe that you and I are an item? Every time we meet we end up arguing. I don't like women who argue. My mother knows that. For God's sake, she's met enough of the women I've dated in the past to know that chalk and cheese just about sums it up when it comes to you and the kind of women I'm attracted to!'

Every word that left his beautiful mouth was a direct hit, but Georgina refused to let him get to her. However, she was distracted enough to ask, with dripping sarcasm, 'So…you don't like women who argue? Or do you mean you don't like women who happen to have an opinion that doesn't concur with yours? In other words, does your attraction to the opposite sex begin and end with towering blondes whose entire vocabulary is comprised of one word… *yes*?'

Matias folded his arms and burst out laughing. 'Now you're making me sound shallow,' he drawled. 'But, just for the record, I've never had a problem with towering blondes with single-syllable vocabularies. When you live life in the fast lane the last thing you want is a sniping nag reminding you that you're back five minutes late and asking where's the milk you were supposed to buy.'

'I doubt you've ever done anything as mundane as buy a pint of milk, Matias.'

'Not recently, I haven't. Not since I was a kid, running errands down to that woefully badly stocked corner shop next to Bertie's place. Of course there was only the occasional need for milk to be *bought*,' he continued, his voice hardening, 'after my parents decided to try their hand with a pet cow. But back on point, here. If my mother has bought this story of yours then she's suffering from more than just mild depression. I mean…when exactly are we supposed to be conducting this raunchy, clandestine relationship that's only now come to light?'

This was the longest one-to-one conversation they had had in a while, and Georgina was mesmerised by his dark, compelling beauty. She was noticing all sorts of details that had only before registered vaguely on her subconscious.

Like the depths of silvery grey in his eyes—at times as icy as the frozen Arctic wastes, at times almost black and smouldering. Like the sensual curve of his mouth and the aquiline perfection of his lean features. Not to mention the dramatic lushness of those black lashes that were so good at shielding what he didn't want the world to see. He oozed an unfair amount of sinful sex appeal, and the longer she looked at him the more addled her brain became and the faster she lost track of what she wanted to say.

As if from those faraway days when she had dreamily fantasised about a relationship that had never stood a chance of materialising, the impact he'd always had on her came rushing back, as though no time had intervened…as though she'd never seen first-hand the type of women he enjoyed and the type he definitely didn't. In short—*her*.

She dragged her disobedient eyes away and focused on a point just past his right shoulder. 'I'm close to your mother, but she doesn't know my every movement, Matias. I told her that we'd been meeting in secret for the past few months but didn't want to bring it out into the open because it was still quite new…'

'Ingenious. But now that's all changed because we've…what? Had an epiphany? Fill in the blanks here, would you?'

'I just said that it was…you know…in the early stages but definitely serious…'

'And I'm guessing that you skirted over the details because you trusted that old adage that people will always believe what they want to believe?'

Georgina blushed. Her green eyes flashed defiance, but she was finding it hard to win him over, and with a sinking heart she knew that he wasn't going to jump on board with this. She would have to return to the village with her tail between her legs and break the news that their so-called serious relationship had crashed and burned.

So much for impulse being a good thing. So much for the ends justifying the means.

'Not going to happen, Georgie,' Matias delivered with finality. 'It was a ludicrous idea and, whilst I appreciate that you lied for the best of reasons, I'm not going to sucked into giving credence to your little charade.'

Defeated, Georgina could only look at him in silence. She tucked her hair behind her ear and sat on her hands, leaning forward, her body rigid with tension.

'Furthermore, I dislike the fact that you saw fit to drag *me* into this poorly thought out scheme of yours. Did it never occur to you that I might have a life planned out that *doesn't* include a phoney relationship with you to appease my mother?'

'No,' Georgina said with genuine honesty, because at the time there had been one thing and one thing only on her mind, and that had been the fastest way to bring Rose back from whatever dark place she was getting lost in.

'Well, perhaps it should have.'

'I just thought—'

'Georgie,' Matias interrupted heavily, standing up to indicate that the conversation was at an end, 'you've always been like my parents. Warm-hearted, but essentially lacking in that practical gene which can sometimes appear harsh but which is the one that makes sense at the end of the day. Now, do you want some fondant?'

'I've lost my appetite. And if by *practical* you mean hard as nails and cold as ice, then I'm very glad that I was born *without* that particular gene.' She stood up as well. 'You may pride yourself, Matias Silva, on seeing the world from your *practical* point of view, but that doesn't necessarily make you a *happy* guy, does it? Yes, it might make you a *wealthy* one, but there's a great big world out here that is rich and rewarding and has nothing to do with how much money you have in your bank account.'

'We'll agree to differ on that one.'

Georgina swerved past him and strode, head held high, towards the front door.

'For God's sake, Georgie, you can still stay the night in my house.'

'I'd rather not, as it happens.'

'Well, where's the B&B?'

'Somewhere in west London—but I'm happy to make my own way there.'

'Just give me the address and I'll get my driver to drop you. It'll be a damn sight more comfortable than trekking on the Underground or trying to work out which bus goes where.'

He didn't give her time to object. He flipped his cell phone out of his pocket and positioned himself in front of the door so that she couldn't run away.

Matias had said what he'd wanted to say but he still felt guilty. He knew that she would see his lack of co-operation in her hare-brained scheme as a lack of concern for his mother. Nothing could be further from the truth. He had never had much in common with his parents—had always seen their idealistic, holistic, hippy approach to life as charming but irresponsible—but that didn't mean that he hadn't loved them in his own way.

His biggest regret was the fact that he hadn't been able to make it back for his father's funeral. He'd been abroad, and it had all happened so damned fast. The flight connections to get him back to Cornwall had not been quick enough. He'd been too late. He'd never had the chance to fix the relationship he'd had with his father—a relationship that had been broken over a period of years as Matias had become ever more distant from his tree-hugging parents, whose ideologies he had never been able to grasp.

He'd failed as a son and, even though he'd spent his adult life trying to make up for it, by assiduously making sure his mother was taken care of, Matias knew that there was a yawning chasm between them for which the small, round, feisty copper-haired woman in front of him had judged and sentenced him a long time ago.

But as far as Matias was concerned involving him in something like this without first consulting him just wasn't on.

'My driver will be here in five minutes.' He looked at her and she squirmed resentfully under his piercing gaze. 'What will you tell my mother?'

'Do you care? Maybe I'll tell her that I showed up here and sadly found you in bed with a blonde.'

She sighed. She had no one but herself to blame for the mess she found herself in. Matias had every right to refuse to go along with her. He had his jam-packed life to lead, after all.

'I won't say that.'

'I didn't think you would.'

'Because I'm so predictable?'

'Because you're not the sort.' He paused. 'I *will* come down to Cornwall,' he murmured thoughtfully. 'Maybe next weekend, and I'll stay for a little longer than I usually do.'

'I'll make sure to keep out of your way,' Georgina inserted politely. 'It might make for fireworks if we're supposed to be in the throes of a hostile break-up.'

Matias looked at her and reluctantly grinned. 'Tell me why you've always been able to make me laugh even though we fight like cat and dog? No, scrap that. You'll probably end up fighting with me again. What story will you spin for my mother when you break the disappointing news that we're no longer a hot item?'

'I don't know. I'll think of something.'

'This was *your* idea,' Matias mused, 'but I'll shoulder the blame for the break-up of a relationship that never was. It'll be far more believable that I'm the baddie in this scenario anyway. I won't be letting my mother down too much.'

He saw the flash of curiosity in her eyes and side-stepped it adroitly.

'Fair's fair, after all. Now… Safe trip back, Georgie.' He hesitated. What else was there to say?

Georgina didn't hang around. His chauffeur-driven Mercedes was waiting by the pavement, engine idling, and she didn't look back as she ducked into the back seat.

Mission Impossible had turned into Mission She Must Have Been Crazy. She consoled herself all way to the bed and breakfast by telling herself that she had done her best and there was nothing more she could have done.

The bed and breakfast was not in the most salubrious of locations, but it was reasonably priced and it was clean. Her room was so small that everything seemed to be squeezed in, with only just enough free space to allow passage from bed to bathroom without minor injuries occurring en route.

She had a shower and stuck on the little tee shirt and skimpy shorts she always wore to sleep. At night, in the darkness of the bedroom…that was the time she felt most self-confident about her body.

She could have been married by now. She could have had a child! It was bizarre to think it, but it was true. Lying there in the dark, something about seeing Matias's dark, beautiful face brought to mind thoughts of Robbie and the marriage that had never been.

They were memories that she kept locked away in her head, but now, like imps released from captivity, they stretched and decided to have a little fun at her expense. Memories of being engaged, planning her big day, only to be told a handful of weeks before they were due to tie the knot that he just couldn't go through with it.

'It's not you!' he had declared magnanimously, in what had to be the most over-used craven expression in any break-up. 'It's me. I just don't feel the same way about you that I used to… I don't understand it…'

They had parted ways and she had had to endure months of sensing the whispered pity behind her back every time she entered a room.

Robbie had stopped being attracted to her. Had he *ever* been attracted to her? Maybe not. Maybe he had been carried along on a tide of wanting to please her parents, because he had been her mother's star pupil.

In her darkest, deepest thoughts she had sometimes wondered whether a part of her hadn't simply been drawn to a guy who was diametrically different from Matias—a guy on whom she could pin all her hopes, finally snuffing out that silly, girlish flame that had continued to burn long after she should have grown out of it.

She cringed when she'd remembered the way Robbie had tried to encourage her to lose a bit of weight. Afterwards, when the dust had settled, she had discovered that he had met and married someone else in record time. Someone long and thin. Ever since then Georgina had made even more of an effort to conceal the body that had let her down.

Yes, it was silly—and, yes, it was nonsensical. But since when did feelings make sense?

She drifted into a restless sleep and had no idea how long she had been asleep when she heard a knocking on her door.

She surfaced, feeling drugged and disorientated. It didn't occur to her to be careful when she tentatively pulled the door open because the bed and breakfast was securely locked against intruders. Which meant that the owner, a lovely woman in her fifties, could be the only person knocking.

And it wasn't that late. Only a little after eleven. But she had been so shattered after her pointless visit to Matias that she had climbed into bed and fallen asleep almost immediately.

Her eyes started at the bottom. Loafers—expensive ones. Black jeans—low-slung. Black close-fitting jumper. Muscular body.

Georgina knew that it was Matias before her eyes collided with his silver dark gaze.

'Let me in, Georgie.'

'What are you doing here?'

'We need to talk.'

'How did you get in? Who let you in?' She peered angrily past him in search of the culprit. 'Whoever let you in had no right to do so!'

'She sensed I wasn't going to steal the family heirlooms. Let me in.'

'Do you know what time it is?'

'*Not* bedtime on a Saturday evening for most people under the age of forty-five. And time for me to tell you that there's been a slight change of plan.'

Matias raked his fingers through his hair and shot her a look of brooding unease.

'Whatever you have to say will have to wait until morning.' Her heart beating like a sledgehammer, and feeling acutely aware of her lack of clothing, Georgina made to shut the door. In response Matias neatly wedged his foot in the open gap before he could be locked out.

'I realise this is not the most convenient place in the world for a conversation, but what I have to say can't wait. My mother called.'

Georgina hesitated. With a sigh, she reluctantly opened the door, then told him to sit at the dressing table so that she could at least get dressed.

She knew the sort he went for. Tall, leggy blondes who weighed next to nothing. She knew that what she had on was no more revealing than what most girls would wear to the park on a hot day. But she still had to swallow down a sickening feeling of self-consciousness as she scuttled into the bathroom clutching jeans and a tee shirt.

She'd disappeared in under ten seconds. But that was all it had taken for Matias to realise that the body she had always been at pains to keep hidden away was voluptuous, with curves in all the right places, and a derriere as round and as perfect as a peach. She wasn't overweight. She was *sexy*.

His libido, which had been sadly tepid during the

last few weeks of his tempestuous relationship with Ava, roared into shocking life, forcing him to conceal a prominent bulge by sitting on a stool by the window.

'You were saying…?' Georgina asked bluntly, when she reappeared in a more acceptable jeans and tee shirt outfit.

She made sure the overhead light was on its brightest setting, so that the room was now as brightly lit as the changing room in a department store. She perched on the edge of the bed, because there were no other available chairs, and rested her hands on her lap.

'You should have dumped your pride and stayed at my place. It's ridiculous what some people call a B&B in London. There's not enough room here to swing a cat.' It was proving impossible for him to get into a comfortable position.

'The owner is lovely. It's cheap. It's clean. And I'm not being ripped off. What did your mother have to say?'

'First of all, I was caught off-guard. It was late, and my mother seldom calls me.'

'That's because she doesn't like to think that she might be disturbing you.'

'More conversations about me, Georgie? Before I could break the disappointing news that we'd decided to call it a day, she launched into a long, excitable congratulatory speech and told me that it was the best thing that had happened to her in a long time.

She said that she was under strict instructions not to call me, to wait until we both came down to Cornwall, but she knew that you'd headed to London and couldn't contain herself. Said she felt she finally had something worth living for...'

'Didn't you believe me when I told you that?'

'Hearing it from the horse's mouth made a difference.'

He stood up, strolled to the window, peered out at an uninspiring view of the back of the building, where tall plastic bins were arranged like soldiers against the wall.

He slowly spun round to look at her, half sat on the broad window ledge. 'You were right. She's the happiest I've heard her in a long time. I couldn't get a word in edgewise.'

'So,' Georgina said slowly, 'what you're saying is that you didn't tell her that it's off...?'

'How could I?'

'That's a bit of a problem, then, isn't it? Considering you told me in no uncertain terms that you weren't going to pretend anything for the sake of your mother.'

Matias flushed darkly. 'Don't think that I *approve* of the way you auditioned me for a role I hadn't applied for,' he reminded her abruptly. 'But here we are. I didn't have the heart to break the bad news down the phone so we'll play this game—but the way I see it this will be a temporary situation. It beggars belief that my mother has fallen for your outrageously improbable scenario, but if it's aiding her recovery then it's something I will have to accept.'

Georgina didn't say anything. She had thought so far and no further when it came to this charade. Now a shiver of unease rippled through her and she looked at Matias from under lowered lashes.

He was the king of urban, sophisticated cool and he was supposed to be going out with *her*. She, too, marvelled that his mother hadn't fainted with disbelief at the improbable scenario.

They were supposed to be an item. Boyfriend and girlfriend. Lovers...

Her stomach lurched, because her imagination threatened to veer off in all sorts of uncharted directions.

'So...' Matias picked up the thread of the conversation. His voice was clipped and businesslike, 'I'm here to briefly discuss the mechanics of this situation. What have you told my mother about us? How much winging it have you done?'

'Can't we discuss this another time?' she replied vaguely.

'Another time?'

'Next week? On the phone, perhaps?'

'Are you living in the real world, Georgie? My mother thinks we're going out with one another in some happy-against-all-odds scenario and you want to discuss the details of our so-called relationship on the phone *next week*? *Maybe?*'

'What are you saying?'

'I'm saying,' Matias imparted coolly, 'that we'll both be leaving for Cornwall in the morning. My mother is expecting us. When we get there, having our stories match up might be an idea.'

'You say that you see this as a temporary situation… do you have a timeline in sight?'

Georgina regretted every second of whatever crazy impulse had plunged her into this mess. It had been a lot easier dealing with a fictional situation. Even when she had boarded that train to London she had not really thought about facing Matias in the flesh. He'd been much easier to deal with in her head. Less intimidating, less forbidding, pretty much less…*everything*.

'I have—and it's not a long one. We go down… we indulge in this charade for a few days… Sooner rather than later things can begin to go downhill. I'm happy to carry the can for the inevitable. There are too many differences between us… It's only become apparent now that we're spending a lot of undiluted time with one another… Put it this way: I can spare a couple of weeks and then I have meetings in the Far East. It would be preferable if all this is sorted before I go.'

'A couple of weeks…' She felt as though she'd hopped on a rollercoaster only to find that it was spinning a lot faster than she'd anticipated.

'I don't see a problem with that.'

'But your mother might be down in the dumps again at the rapid demise of our relationship.'

'Which is something you should have considered before you had your light bulb moment. We could hash all this out on the drive down tomorrow, but I think it better if we cover the basics now. I'm going to have to work for the majority of the trip, bearing in mind I'll be leaving the office without warning.'

'You're going to *work* while you drive?'

'Of course not, Georgie! My driver will take us and I'll work in the back. You can bring a book, or some knitting, or whatever you need to occupy your time. We can fine-tune our stories just before we reach my mother's house.'

He fixed his amazing eyes on her and Georgina had the curious sensation of free falling. Her stomach lurched and swooped as her eyes drifted down to his mouth and then immediately skittered away. She licked her lips and croaked some nonsense about having some work to do for her next job.

'Right,' he said, as her voice tapered off, 'how is it that we've gone from war zone to bedroom in such a short space of time?'

'I haven't thought through the details,' she admitted. 'I suppose we can say it was just one of those things. Opposites attracting. It happens. I mean, *you* have a long history of being attracted to women who are nothing like you.'

'Nor are they like *you*,' he inserted smoothly. 'Aside from which, I've never had a serious relationship with any of them—not like the one we're supposed to be having...'

'I acted on impulse,' Georgina said in a muted voice. 'I would never normally think of deceiving anyone, but before I could think things through—work out how it's even credible that the two of us could ever have anything going—I'd come right out and spun a story. I'm sorry about that. You've been cornered into doing something you don't want to do, and I don't blame you if you're seething.'

'Forget it.' Matias looked at her.

'I never even stopped to think that you might actually be going out with someone…one of your ditzy blondes…'

'You were so wrapped up in cheering up my mother that rational thought took a back seat?'

'Something like that.'

'So, it's a very good thing that I'm going to be in charge of making sure that that doesn't happen again. We will do what is necessary and make sure that the boundary lines are firmly in place.'

'Meaning…?' Georgina automatically bristled.

Matias didn't say anything for a few taut seconds. Out of the blue he was thinking back to that luscious body—a body he would never have guessed lay beneath the layers of unattractive flowing sacks she was so fond of wearing. His libido kicked into gear again and he scowled.

'Meaning we don't forget that this is a convenient charade…'

There was no way Matias was going to give in to that sudden, inexplicable surge in his libido. When it came to relationships Georgina White was after the real thing. Once upon a time she'd been engaged, and she'd been stood up at the last minute. That didn't mean she'd shut the door on her dreams. That wasn't her nature. But she'd been hurt once. There was no way he would ever be responsible for hurting her again by taking what his libido had wanted when he'd seen her in those next-to-nothing pyjamas.

'I won't forget,' Georgina returned stiffly. 'And once again I apologise for landing you in this mess. Your life is so well ordered—this must be a nightmare for you to take in.'

'Now, why do I sense an implied insult behind that butter-wouldn't-melt-in-your-mouth remark?' Matias drawled, glancing at her full lips and absently noting how perfectly defined they were. Like rosebuds the colour of crushed raspberries. Funny he'd never noticed that before...

He lifted his dark eyes to hers. 'I really wouldn't waste time regretting what you've done. What's the point? The fact is that we're here now...in this together for better or for worse, so to speak.'

'I didn't stop to think things through.' Georgina chewed her lip and shot him a worried glance. 'I never considered the ramifications of how your mother would feel when it all...you know...collapsed...'

'That's a bridge to be crossed when we get to it. You're projecting ahead. She'll be fine.' He looked at her, his dark eyes brooding. 'At least once it's over she'll be able to think that I'm capable of holding down a relationship with a woman who isn't obsessed with her physical appearance.'

'Until you return to your catwalk model blondes,' Georgina pointed out absently.

He shot her a crooked grin that did all sorts of annoying things to her heart-rate. Had she spent her entire life oblivious to just how spectacular Matias was? she wondered. No, that wasn't it. She'd always known just how spectacular he was. It was just that now the situation between them was leading her to think thoughts that were taboo—wicked thoughts about what that lean, muscular body might look like underneath his clothes.

A Pandora's box was opening and she knew that she had to make sure it stayed shut. She wasn't an impressionable teenager any more! And, as he had coolly pointed out, this was a charade—a piece of fiction with no basis in reality.

'Maybe I'll go for a different type next time round,' he drawled, standing up. He stretched, flexed his muscles and strolled towards the door.

'What about all these details you want to put into place before tomorrow?' Georgina remained where she was. 'I thought you rushed over here to iron everything out because you're going to work in the car on the way down?'

His hand was on the doorknob as he turned to look at her thoughtfully. 'Question: did you ask for the house tour because you needed some background information to consolidate the myth that we've been meeting secretly, and it would have seemed odd if my mother had asked you about my house and drawn a blank?'

Georgina reddened, and then nodded sheepishly, at which Matias burst out laughing.

'You're one of a kind, Georgie,' he mused, rocking on his heels and looking at her in silence for long enough for her to start feeling hot and bothered. 'And one of a kind is certainly going to be a novelty for me.'

He opened the door. 'I'll text you before I leave tomorrow to come and fetch you. And then our little adventure will begin…'

CHAPTER THREE

HE'D PHONED TO SAY he would be there at two sharp, and right on time Matias arrived to collect her. He didn't leave the car, instead choosing to phone her mobile and then wait, working in the back seat of the Mercedes, while she settled the bill and exchanged a few pleasantries with the owner.

It was another lovely day. Summer was promising never to end and Georgina wished that she had brought something other than the long skirt she had worn the day before and a change of top.

Shielding her eyes from the glare of the sun, she walked briskly towards the one and only car on the road she knew had to be his because it was the one and only car that had tinted windows and looked as though it had been driven straight from a showroom. She stepped into air-conditioned cool and shut the door behind her.

Knowing that her plan was in danger of being put into action, she had spent what had remained of the night tossing and turning and projecting into the future. Matias had made it sound easy. They'd appear together, they'd begin to argue, they'd break up and lo and behold everything would be done and dusted in two weeks, leaving a saddened but more upbeat Rose who would no longer be prone to depression.

Georgina was uneasily aware that she might have bitten off more than she could chew, and that the easily digestible scenario Matias had painted might turn into a horrendous nightmare. But he had come on board and it was too late to back out now.

She met his eyes as she shuffled to find a comfortable position next to him while strapping herself in. Suddenly she was lost for words, and shy in a way she never had been before in his presence.

'I've had a few hours to think about this,' he opened without preamble, snapping shut his computer and fixing her with his amazing silver-grey eyes.

He slid shut the partition separating his driver from them for privacy.

'Have you had a change of mind?' she asked,

'On the contrary,' Matias drawled. 'If you knew me at all, you'd know that once I make my mind up on a certain course of action I stick to it. Which brings me to what I was thinking about after I left you.'

'Which was what?'

The car had slid silently away from the kerb, and with the tinted windows and the lack of noise she felt cocooned in a luxurious bubble. The outside world had ceased to exist. From his house to his car, every single aspect of him oozed extreme wealth. No one would ever guess that he came from a working class background where luxuries had been few and far between.

'However weirdly unquestioning my mother has been about the details of our so-called relationship, she's not stupid. She does know me, and she knows that it's unlikely that I would suddenly be attracted to someone who doesn't at the very least make an effort to dress properly.'

A slow wash of colour rushed to her cheeks and Georgina felt a swell of rage. 'What are you trying to say?'

'You know what I'm trying to say. Flowing skirts? Baggy tops? Shoes made for hiking in rough terrain?'

'Do you have *any* idea how rude you're being right now?' she said tightly.

'You have my sincere apologies—'

'I'm a food photographer.' She ignored the token lip service he had paid, trying to placate her. Her voice was cold and steely. 'I'm freelance. There's no need for me to have a wardrobe of power suits and cocktail outfits.'

'Which is exactly why we won't be heading for that section of Selfridges.'

'What are you talking about? Why would we be going to Selfridges?' The rollercoaster sensation was back with a vengeance. 'I'm not following you.'

'If we're going to do this, then we're going to do it properly, Georgie. No half-measures. We need to be convincing. The alternative is that my mother suspects it's all a crock of lies and her health is set back even more than before. She will lose trust in both of us.'

Georgina didn't say anything because he was painting a graphic picture. He was also making her realise just how sketchy she had been when she had told that first little white lie.

'We might be able to gloss over the little technicality that we've previously spent most of our time together engaged in a series of low-level arguments... We might just be able to pull off that old chestnut of—as you've said—opposites attracting. But beyond that the details have to carry some verisimilitude.'

And after a long line of catwalk models, Georgina thought furiously, *it would beggar belief that he would go for someone who didn't think twice about snapping up bargain buys in the clothes section of a supermarket.*

'Well, what about *you* dressing down?' she fired back.

'For example...?' he returned smoothly, with an undercurrent of amusement in his voice.

'Well, less of the designer cool and more of the beach bum!'

'Interesting thought.' He sat back, leaning against the car door, his legs sprawled apart, one hand resting loosely on his thigh. 'What would that be? Ill-fitting flowered shirt? Cheap shorts? Flip-flops? Is that the kind of look you would go for?'

Georgina blushed and looked away. The man was so good-looking that he would pull off a bin bag and he knew it. Hence the smile that made her want to grind her teeth together in frustration.

'No one would ever believe that you would wear anything as casual as flowered shirts and flip-flops, Matias. Even when you're relaxing you give the impression that you'd really rather be working.'

'I had no idea you could be so accurate when it came to reading me. Maybe there's more substance to our relationship than meets the eye...'

'We don't *have* a relationship—and I won't be dressing like that woman you dispatched yesterday.'

'I'm shocked you're not kicking up more of a fight over this,' Matias admitted with honesty.

'Is that what you think I do? Kick up a fight over everything?'

That stung for some reason, because there was an element of truth in it. She knew that she picked at him, but she quickly told herself that he deserved it. He hardly ever came down to visit his mother...he always made it abundantly clear that he had moved on and was bored with the place he came from...he hadn't even shown up to his dad's funeral!

And yet so much about him refused to be corralled into neat little boxes.

'Not everything,' Matias conceded. 'At least not in the company of other people. I've seen you laugh, so I know that when it comes to picking fights I'm the special one in your life. I get the folded arms and the scowls.' He grinned, watched her colour rise, perversely enjoying it.

'We've had our differences...' Georgina could feel her cheeks suffused with colour. 'But it's only because I've always been close to your parents.' She hesitated, then found herself confiding, 'I adored mine, of course, but I didn't have loads in common with them. I liked art and taking pictures and rummaging in the undergrowth. And you know my parents, Matias...they were all about intellectual pursuits. I think they pretty much packed it in with me when I hit my teens.'

This was something Georgina had never confessed to anyone, and she was surprised that she was confessing it now—especially to Matias—but then wasn't that part and parcel of his compelling personality? So cool, so controlled, so *annoying*. And yet...and yet...he could engage with her on levels no other man she had ever met had been able to.

'Meaning...?'

Georgina laughed, and that did something to Matias's libido again, reminded him of those sexy, unexpected little curves he had glimpsed the night before.

'I stopped getting big, thick books for birthday presents,' she said drily, 'and my mum stopped slipping law, international politics and university into the conversation.'

'I never knew you were bothered by that,' Matias murmured, an element of surprise in his voice.

'A bit. But they were great when it came to supporting my decision to go into photography.'

'Taking pictures of my parents' produce…?'

'It was a start, Matias. I have a steady stream of work now, but I can't afford to splash out on a new wardrobe of clothes I'll only be wearing for two minutes.'

'I wouldn't dream of letting you put your hand in your pocket to buy *anything*,' he said flatly.

Their eyes collided and her heart skipped a beat. Heat rushed through her body and her mouth went dry. He really was so very beautiful. That raven-black hair curling at the nape of his neck, the sensuality of his mouth, the lazy intensity of his eyes…

'And if,' he continued, 'my mother suspected that you had, she would know for sure that this is a sham—because no woman of mine has ever been expected to pay for anything when I'm around.'

But I'm not your woman, Georgina thought confusedly.

'And she would know that you'd bought your own clothes because you wouldn't be able to resist buying items that are two sizes too big.'

'That's out of order!'

Matias laughed. 'Entirely,' he murmured, 'but what's the point in tiptoeing round the issue? Sexy, but refined is the image I'm thinking you should go for.'

Georgina blanched. In what world could she go from homely to *sexy, but refined*?

Aghast, she realised that while they had been talking the driver had been skilfully manoeuvring through the London traffic and had now pulled to a smooth stop at the back of the expensive department store.

She was channelled out of the car and shepherded to the designer floor where, somehow, a personal shopper had been summoned to assist them.

'I'll sit in on this,' Matias said, *sotto voce*. 'If we're going to do this then, like I said, we're going to do it well. And it starts with clothes.'

He sat on a velvet-upholstered sofa with every semblance of keen interest. He didn't even open his computer. He watched in silence as clothes were brought out for inspection—clothes that she would, presumably, wear for him.

He watched as she resentfully paraded in them, chucking aside anything that looked too small, too short or too tight or showed off her boobs too much. Because *he* might go for that look, but Rose would know in an instant that *she* never would.

She opted for *refined* over *sexy*, and she did her utmost to ignore those lazily inspecting eyes as she tried to douse the hot fires of her embarrassment.

Eventually, when the pile of clothes had grown to a ridiculous amount, she put her foot down and resurfaced in her original outfit, hands on her hips and grim determination on her face.

'That's it,' she said flatly. 'I'm not getting anything else.'

'Why not?'

The assistant had vanished to start the business of packaging all the clothes, and Matias patted the space next to him on the sofa—which Georgina ignored.

'I thought women enjoyed nothing more than buying clothes.'

'Not me.' Georgina stood in front of him, arms folded.

'So you hated every second of the experience?'

Georgina hesitated. She refused to admit that a part of her had rather *liked* the business of trying on stuff she would never normally have worn, a lot of which hadn't looked half bad. And a forbidden part of her whispered that trying on stuff *for him* had made the experience even more exhilarating.

'It was a necessary ordeal,' she offered in a clipped voice.

Matias laughed shortly, unfazed. 'Liar. Well, you're going to have to up the appreciation levels,' he drawled, 'and eliminate the sniping rejoinders if we're going to be playing to the gallery.'

He stood up just as the assistant reappeared, obediently waiting in the background for his imperious beckoning finger.

'But you're right. There's enough there to be going on with. It's not as though this little play-acting game is destined to be a never-ending charade.'

Georgina followed his eyes to the expensively ribboned, tissue-wrapped pile of packages on the table by the assistant.

There were clothes and shoes for every conceivable occasion. For expensive meals out…for casual dining in his mother's garden—he had informed her that he would be getting a top caterer in for the duration of his stay with her—for walks along the beach, with his mother doubtless tripping along with them as witness to their rosy relationship.

Before, presumably, it all began going sour.

Georgina wondered whether they should have got a few special *it's all going pear-shaped* outfits. And then she thought that at that point she would just slip back into her normal gear and that would say it all.

'You'll have to show up wearing one of these outfits we've bought,' he said, without glancing at her as he paid for the pile of clothes. Transaction done, he turned to her. 'I'm thinking that your mystery visits to London, under cover of darkness, would have entailed something of your new persona being presented as my new and exciting love interest. In short, would you have turned up in London wearing comfy work clothes and shoes designed to take on rough terrain and stamp it into submission?'

'I honestly don't know how I'm going to look as though you're the light of my life,' Georgina muttered through gritted teeth, but she did as told, peeking into one parcel and then disappearing into the changing room.

She had made sure, during the clothes parade, to keep some of her own baggy clothes on—the flowing skirt twinned with a smaller top, the loose-fitting top twinned with slim-fitting trousers... But now, when she appeared a few minutes later, she was wearing a complete outfit, and she looked...

Matias tried not to gape. The woman looked stunning. The girl next door was gone. In her place was a woman any red-blooded man would have wanted to haul off to the nearest bed, caveman-style.

He sat forward. Slowly. He knew he was staring but he couldn't help himself. She was wearing pin-striped silk culottes and a small silk top, and the ensemble managed to leave everything to the imagination while sending his libido into the stratosphere.

She had had her hair scraped back before, but now it was loose, tumbling over her shoulders in colourful curls. The practical sandals had been replaced with soft leather flats.

'You look...pretty good.' Matias stood up with fluid grace and nodded at the assistant to bring the bags, while keeping his eyes riveted to Georgina for a few seconds.

'Thanks.'

She knew that she was blushing. He was looking at her, for the first time, in the way a man would look at a woman. So *pretty good* might not the compliment of a lifetime, but then this was a game they were playing. It wasn't as though he was really attracted to her. But she was no longer invisible...

She reached for her backpack but he swept it up before she could fetch it.

'We forgot about a handbag.' He turned to the assistant and told her to get something in tan, price no object. 'There's no place in this charade for...' he dangled her backpack from two fingers '...*this*.'

Georgina thought that was more like it. A brisk, businesslike approach to the situation foisted upon him. *Bye-bye scruffy backpack—hello co-ordinating designer handbag.* It was a timely reminder that when he had stared at her, sending her blood pressure soaring, it hadn't been because he was *seeing her*—not really. He had been evaluating her, to work out whether or not she fitted the bill for the part she was playing.

She had felt a frisson, the feathery brush of excitement as those fabulous eyes had rested on her, but there was no need to hear any alarm bells. He didn't fancy her and she certainly didn't fancy him. And even if she did—if she found her eyes straying and getting a little lost in those sinfully exotic good looks—then her reaction was perfectly normal, driven by her hormones and not her head. He was stupidly sexy and she was, after all, a normal healthy woman.

But he'd never been her type and—especially after Robbie and the way she'd been dumped—she had sworn off men. If someone came into her life—someone solid and stable, with a dash of creativity... someone she could envisage sharing her life with—

then all well and good. But she would never again be drawn to someone inappropriate.

Robbie had been inappropriate. He had always expected her to bow to his greater knowledge and compliment him on his achievements. He'd been smart and well-read and intellectual, and she hadn't stopped to look any further because she'd been in love with the idea of being love.

The drive down to Cornwall was not the awkward situation she had anticipated.

Matias, confirming what he had said to her, worked for much of the journey, only surfacing when they were a matter of twenty minutes away from his mother's house, at which point he briefly quizzed her on what, exactly, she had told her mother.

'Not a huge amount,' she admitted. 'It was a spur-of-the-moment thing and I came to London almost immediately to see you.'

'I still find it difficult to credit that you could have made such a monumental decision on the spur of the moment,' Matias murmured.

'Don't you do anything on impulse?'

'What do *you* think?'

'I think it's really strange. Your parents must be the most impulsive couple I've ever known, especially compared to mine, and yet you're completely the opposite. Look at the way they embarked on their organic farming…and the way your mother took up Reiki…and then there was the whole horses for the disabled business…such a shame that crashed and burned.'

'And yet anyone could have predicted that that would be a mistake.'

His knew his voice had cooled somewhat. He could remember his mother passing round her cut-price *Reiki at Home* business cards to some of the parents at his boarding school at the end of term, having rocked up in their brightly painted camper van, much to the hilarity of all the boys in the entire school.

'I certainly did and I was barely out of my teens at the time. As for doing anything on impulse? They're a successful argument for *avoiding* impulsive behaviour.'

What Georgina saw as romantic and glamorous, he saw as a regrettable handicap.

'Maybe,' Matias continued, 'if they'd started with the organic farming from the very beginning and specialised in it, it might have gone further than it did. But instead they got waylaid by anything and everything, and naturally a Jack-of-all-trades-and-master-of-none will always be destined to fail.'

'They were *happy*. They didn't *fail*.'

Matias grunted, disinclined to continue a conversation that was going nowhere. 'So, no stories we need to tally?' He brought the conversation back to the matter at hand. 'No eyes meeting across a crowded dance floor? Good. The fewer lies, the less room for complications.'

'And the quicker the inevitable end to our relationship?'

Georgina marvelled at his ability to see everything in black and white. No surprise there, but once again it made her realise how different they were. For some reason that was a reassuring thought, and she held on to it because it stopped her disobedient imagination from getting out of hand.

'Should we plan that out now?'

'No need to muddy the waters just yet. You can leave that to me. Like I said, I'll take the hit.'

They were approaching Rose's house, much to Georgina's surprise, because the drive seemed to have been completed in the blink of an eye. They had already passed the turning that led to her parents' house, which she was looking after and living in rent-free while they were in Australia. The houses had given way to open fields on one side and on the other a distant view of the sea.

Rose's house sat on a hill, and Georgina felt as if she was seeing for the first time just how little enthusiasm the older woman now had for the fields she and Antonio had spent years cultivating. The crops looked vaguely straggly and ill-kempt. There was even a feeling of dilapidation about the house, as they approached it, although that shouldn't be the case because a lot of money had been spent on it over time, thanks to Matias.

'It looks tired,' Matias pointed out, reading her mind. 'I've tried persuading my mother that it would

be in her interests to move to something more man-
ageable but she won't be budged.'

'Many happy memories within those four walls,'
Georgina murmured, surprising Matias, because that
emotional explanation would never have occurred
to him.

His brain just didn't function along those lines. He
didn't see the house in the same way at all. He'd been
out of it for such a long time that when he looked all
he saw was concrete and glass and a bunch of prob-
lems waiting to happen.

Rose was waiting for them when they pulled up
outside. A semi-circular courtyard fronted the property and the front door was open, framing Rose, who
was beaming from ear to ear.

She was a slightly built woman, with soft fair
hair that she was allowing to turn grey. She had
enormous blue eyes and the sort of delicate features
that had once made her startlingly pretty but now
made her look fragile and breakable, as though a
single gust of wind might blow her off her feet and
whip her away.

But she was still smiling as she hurried forward,
peppering them with questions, then standing back
to look at them both with excitement and satisfaction. She moved to embrace Matias—a proper tight
hug of an embrace—and Georgina noted the way
he stiffened before returning the embrace with awkward sincerity.

He's not used to such shows of affection, she

thought, startled. But then she wondered why she was surprised, when she knew how distant the relationship between them was—when she had seen with her own two eyes the awkward way they circled one another, almost as though they had forgotten how to interact as mother and son. It seemed, with that spontaneous hug, that it was a chasm Rose was trying to close.

Matias had moved to stand by Georgina, and then he did something both expected and unexpected at one and the same time.

He slung his arm over her shoulders.

Just like that her breasts were suddenly heavy, her nipples pinched and sensitive, scraping against her cotton bra. She wanted to squirm, to *move*, because she was gripped by a sudden restlessness. But instead she remained as still as a statue, barely able to breathe as he absently stroked just below her collarbone in small circles, finding bare skin beneath the light silk top.

She knew that Rose was chatting animatedly as they walked into the cool of the house. She was aware of Matias responding. But the details were foggy because all she could think of was Matias's arm still around her, so close to her breast, his fingers so close to her rigid, aching nipples.

'I think,' she heard him drawl in that deep, dark, velvety voice of his, 'that I'll leave Georgie to answer that one…'

'Huh?' Georgina blinked vaguely and accepted

the cup of tea that had appeared in front of her. She looked at Matias and her heart banged in her chest. Her pulses raced and her pupils dilated.

'How did we meet? My mother wants no details spared.'

Georgina had not taken any physical contact into consideration. But to all intents and purposes they were here together in Cornwall, a couple, doing all the things most normal couples did.

Like putting their arms around one another.

Like *this*…she thought, with sluggish fascination as Matias lowered his head.

Her eyes closed and her mouth parted as his lips ever so lightly brushed against hers.

The kiss was over in a heartbeat, but the effect was devastating. She blinked and made a huge effort to get her brain to engage. His attention was back on his mother, and Georgina was furious with herself for letting the kiss get to her. But it had been thrilling. She didn't know whether that was because it was forbidden or because he was such a good kisser that he'd managed to blow her self-control to smithereens.

She edged away from him and sat down in front of the cup of tea which she had deposited on the table. Rose followed suit while Matias strolled through the kitchen, inspecting stuff.

'So?' Rose was pressing. 'How *did* the pair of you meet? Silly me! I know you've known one another since for ever, but when did you first realise…? Oh, I would never have guessed!'

She was tripping excitedly over her words and thankfully not pausing for breath, which meant that Georgina hadn't been cornered into answering any direct questions yet—although she knew that it was just a matter of time.

'You've certainly kept it under your hat, Georgie! I had no idea you were going up and down to London, seeing Matias!'

'The train service is so efficient, so quick…' Georgina said faintly.

'And I can understand,' Rose exclaimed, 'when Matias says that neither of you wanted to say anything yet *just in case*…'

'Ah…er…yes…' Georgina's eyes skittered towards Matias, who raised his eyebrows, sipped his tea and left her floundering in her own panicked witlessness. 'Well, you know…relationships can be so unpredictable…'

'Of course, my darling. And you of all people would know that after Robbie. I'm sure you were ultra-cautious…'

'Yes, ultra-cautious,' Georgina parroted weakly.

'But you did the right thing,' Rose mused thoughtfully. 'Instead of rushing into a replacement relationship you took lots of time to come to terms with what had happened before dipping your toes back into the dating pool.'

She gazed at her son with affection.

'Darling,' she addressed him, 'I can't begin to tell you how I hoped…' Her voice threatened to break and she gathered herself. 'But you still haven't told me how all this *happened*. Was it as romantic as it sounds?'

Matias fixed his fabulous eyes on Georgina and said precisely what she'd hoped he wouldn't say.

'Darling—would you like to do the honours?'

He was such a good actor, Georgina thought with some of her usual spirit. The warm voice, the light touch, the easy proximity... He was probably thinking of the next big deal he had to complete while playing the attentive lover, but no one would ever have guessed—least of all his mother, who looked as though Christmas had come early.

She gathered herself and smiled brightly. 'Of course...*darling*...'

Busying herself pouring another cup of tea killed a couple of minutes, during which time Matias sauntered towards the kitchen table, where she had sat down, and rested his hands lightly on her shoulders. He gently massaged the nape of her neck, then lifted her hair to feather a kiss where his massaging thumbs had been.

Breathing became difficult. This was totally out of order, she thought furiously. Some semblance of affection might be permissible, but *this*...?

'What was it,' he murmured, thankfully straightening, although he kept his hands on her shoulders, 'that made you fall head over heels in love with me?'

'No idea.' Georgina lightly covered his hands with hers and gently but firmly prised herself free.

In response, Matias circled around to take the seat facing her, slightly behind his mother so that he could watch the expression on her face without Rose being any the wiser.

Georgina ignored him to the best of her ability. She smiled at Rose, although her jaw was beginning to ache from the effort of pretending that this was just a normal conversation.

Out of the corner of her eye, she registered Matias's lazy gaze resting on her. Was this his way of punishing her for having put him in a situation he hadn't invited? Watching her having to flesh out the little white lie that had propelled him into sitting here in his mother's kitchen, pretending to be someone he wasn't?

Rose was looking at her with eager, interested eyes and Georgina felt a flash of anger towards Matias. Couldn't he see that he was making their inevitable break-up all the harder by laying on the touchy-feely stuff in such abundance?

She gathered herself. 'I mean, it certainly wasn't his engaging humility or his sweet-natured, easygoing personality! You know your son, Rose! He's challenging, to say the least! And sometimes…' she smiled brightly at Matias '…I'd go so far as to say there's an arrogant streak there…'

Matias watched, amused, and then he returned with a wicked smile, 'Well, my darling, if it wasn't my soft, soppy nature and my ambitious streak, it must have been my scintillating and exciting personality… wouldn't you agree?'

How, she wondered irritably, had *sweet-natured and easy-going* turned into *soft and soppy*? How had *arrogant and challenging* become *ambitious*?

'Let's just say,' he continued, much to his mother's delight—this was obviously just the sort of familiar banter she enjoyed hearing—'that I made her heart race and it hasn't stopped racing since. Wouldn't you say, my darling, that that just about sums it up...?'

CHAPTER FOUR

'THAT,' GEORGINA SAID less than an hour later, once Rose had retired for a brief rest before dinner— which she had prepared even though Matias had told her not to bother, that he would make sure a caterer was on board when they arrived, 'was awful.'

'You look as though you could do with a drink.' He poured them both a glass of wine and then stood back to look at her coolly. 'I had my doubts about this hare-brained idea of yours, but I have to admit that my mother is a different woman to the one I visited three months ago.'

Georgina accepted the proffered glass of wine and stared moodily into the clear liquid as she swirled it round and round and wondered how a couple of hours spent with a woman she dearly loved could end up being as wearying as if she'd run a marathon up Mount Everest carrying weights.

But the questions had been exhaustive and had called for a repertoire of invention she had not foreseen when she had embarked on—as Matias had called it—her *hare-brained scheme*.

When did they first know…? Where did they go when they met…? Had they met in Cornwall on the sly…? What about getting engaged…? Summer wedding or winter…? What sort of rings did she like…? There was an excellent jewellers not too far away— she knew the one… Oh, don't mind me…you probably think I'm getting ahead of myself…

By the time the conversation had settled into something resembling normality Georgina had been wrung out. And Matias hadn't helped matters.

'I didn't appreciate your hands all over me,' she bristled now, sipping her wine and hunching into herself as she looked at him severely over the rim of her glass. 'I know it's important that we maintain a…a…realistic…er…front, but you don't have to touch me all the time!'

'Point taken,' Matias said piously. 'Although I thought you might welcome the way I've thrown myself into this situation without grumbling.'

'And is there really any need for us to go exploring tomorrow?'

'What do you suggest we do, as a loved-up couple with stars in their eyes?' Matias returned coolly. 'Go our separate ways and communicate via email while I'm here? Don't forget that I didn't *ask* to get embroiled in this situation but here I am. Rather, here *we* are. I propose you go with the flow and cut back on the steady stream of objections.'

It still got on his nerves that he was doing something he hadn't banked on doing—especially something he hadn't generated himself. But Matias had enjoyed himself this evening. His mother's attitude towards him had been subtly but noticeably different. Less...*wary*. It surprised him how much he had liked the unexpected thaw when he'd always considered himself as hard as nails when it came to accepting the shortcomings of his relationship with his mother.

He'd always known that she judged him for the life choices he had made and, crucially, for not being able to attend his father's funeral. But, despite that, their relationship had meandered along, with neither party doing the other any harm. He'd fulfilled every obligation when it came to supporting his mother financially. Whatever she wanted, big or small, he did not hesitate to provide. And if there was a certain distance between them, then Matias accepted that it was simply the way it was. Irreversible and inevitable and not that unusual when it came to family dynamics.

Except it wasn't.

His mother had embraced him. She had teased him. Had laughed with genuine warmth. Her guarded affection had been replaced with an open show of love and it had felt like the reconnection he had never imagined possible.

And as for the touching that Georgina had talked about... He'd liked that as well.

She wasn't bony, like the catwalk models he was accustomed to dating. Her skin was soft and smooth, and those intermittent touches had put him in mind of what it might feel like to touch a *real* woman— which was a phrase he would have scoffed at only days ago.

He *liked* the smallness and the roundness of her... he liked the way her breasts were generous and lush...he liked the shapeliness of her legs. Touching her had *definitely* not been a hardship.

'Your mother doesn't expect us to be all over one another!' Georgina was protesting now, heatedly.

'She didn't look distraught at the sight.'

'Well, I won't be joining you for dinner tonight.' She stood up and primly smoothed her hands over her trousers. 'I have stuff to do.'

'Stuff? What *stuff*?'

'None of your business.'

'Oh, but *everything's* my business now that we're a couple...'

'You're enjoying this, aren't you?' Georgina gritted.

Matias delivered a cool, mocking smile. *'Enjoying?'*

Georgina flushed, because of course he wouldn't be *enjoying* anything. He'd been shoved into playing a part with a woman who got on his nerves most of the time and whom he didn't fancy at all. He would rather steer clear of her. Instead, where was he? Having to put on a show of physical affection for the sake of his mother.

'I have a job coming up,' she said, opting for a conciliatory tone. 'I'm photographing some food for an

up-and-coming young local chef. It's a good job because she's going to be using some of your mother's
produce—that should be free advertising for the farm.
I need to start working on my templates.'

Matias grimaced. 'I've never seen your work,' he
mused. 'I'll have to put that right. And, for the record, while I'm here I'm going to use the opportunity
to try and persuade my mother to leave this house.
It's too big. Naturally there are memories, but isn't
that what photo albums are all about?'

Georgina shot him an incredulous look from
under her lashes. 'You're *impossible*, Matias. How
can you be so cold and unfeeling? Not that anyone
would guess with that touchy-feely show you put on
for your mother. You're a brilliant actor. But… I'm
really glad you can see a difference in your mum. I
know you got dragged into this, and it helps that you
can see why I ended up doing what I did. Anyway…'

She stood up and hovered for a few minutes.

'I'm going to head off now, before Rose comes
down. She'll understand. She knows that I have a
lot of prepping to do before the shoot the day after
tomorrow.'

She hovered some more. She hesitated for just a
little too long. Watching him. Paralysed by the sur-
real nature of events, torn by weird, conflicting emotions that she couldn't rationalise.

The sound of Rose's voice made her start.

'You're going? But, my darling, *where* are you
going?'

It took a few moments for Georgina's brain to sluggishly register that Rose, who should have been safely tucked up having a nap, was now looking at her and waiting for an answer.

The only thing Georgina could stammer out in response was, 'Home. You know…work… But of course I'll be back tomorrow…'

'What Georgie is trying to say…' Matias neatly stepped into the breach, moving to gather her against him '…is that she's going home to finish up what she has to do but she'll be joining us for dinner.'

'Er…' Georgina's voice trailed off.

'Darling,' Rose intercepted briskly, 'I'll have none of this nonsense about you two being apart while you're down here. Never you mind my sensibilities! I wasn't born a century ago! I do realise that young people in love actually share beds! You could have Matias's bedroom here, but I think you might enjoy the privacy of staying at *your* place, Georgie.'

She beamed and Georgina tried hard to beam back and appear delighted.

'You don't want a middle-aged woman getting underfoot.'

'Er…but… Matias…? Didn't you say that the whole point of you coming down here was to see your mum?'

'And I will,' Matias soothed with infuriating calm. 'But of course my mother is right. It makes complete sense for us to be in the same place.'

He moved to give his mother a peck on the cheek.

She looked delighted. While she, Georgina, contemplated a scenario she hadn't banked on in a million years.

Share a house? With Matias?

On the one hand at least she would be able to dispatch him to the furthest bedroom from hers, because his mother wouldn't be there keeping tabs on the loving couple, but still…

Share a house?

'You look a little anxious, Georgie.'

Rose stepped forward to reach for Georgina's hands, which she clasped warmly. Her sharp eyes reminded Georgina that recoiling in horror at the prospect of sharing her space with the guy she was supposed to adore wasn't going to do.

'But I do understand that you want to finish some work tonight—and, yes, give Matias some time to be on his own here with me.' She looked at Matias with a smile. 'That's the sort of lovely, understanding girl Georgie is. Always putting other people ahead of herself.'

'An absolute angel,' Matias murmured, tightening his hand on her waist and giving it an affectionate little squeeze that made her stiffen in response.

'Perhaps tomorrow you two can go off and do something exciting together. It's so beautiful around here at this time of year! I know you probably think you should drag me along wherever you go, but please don't.' Her face shadowed for a few seconds, but then the smile returned. 'Why don't you head to

Padstow and explore? I could even make you a picnic to take to the beach. When was the last time you were at a beach, Matias?'

She looked at her son, tentative and affectionate at the same time, breaking new ground, making Georgina feel that it would be a sin to rain on the older woman's parade.

'A century and a half ago…' he drawled.

So it was decided. The details of this wonderful day out floated around Georgina's head. She tried to think *It's all for a good cause—just look at how great Rose looks compared to a few days ago...* Instead, the only thing she had in her head was an image of Matias in her house, in a bedroom, in the shower… sharing her space. An intruder in her life and one *she* had invited—an intruder who could make her break out in a cold sweat and remind her of a time when she had idolised the ground he walked on.

Eventually Rose left the room, and the first thing Matias said, dropping his arms and walking away from her, was, 'Do I make you nervous? Because you were behaving like a cat on a hot tin roof just then.'

'Of *course* you don't make me nervous.' Georgina cleared her throat and let loose a brittle laugh, very conscious of the burning patch of skin he had touched and of those amazing eyes now pinned to her face. 'I just didn't expect your mother to…to…'

'To suggest we actually do what most people would do, given they were in a serious relationship? Inhabit the same bedroom?'

Georgina squirmed and reddened. 'I thought she would be…might be…relieved not to have to confront that…er…reality… Plus, how are we to demonstrate the decline in our relationship if your mother isn't around to witness it?'

'Did you think the occasional woman I've brought here over the years was primly shown to a bedroom on another floor when I came to visit? And as for my mother seeing first-hand all the differences between us… Well, there will be time enough to demonstrate those. In the meanwhile, this is a tonic for her and I have no intention of whipping it away just yet.'

'You're not exactly being helpful, Matias.' Georgina drew in a sharp, impatient breath and he raised his eyebrows.

'Nor are you,' Matias responded, without skipping a beat. 'If concern for my mother is top of your agenda, then you should be embracing her enthusiasm for us to spend all our available time down here together, instead of trying to figure out how fast you can disillusion her.'

'That's a far cry from you refusing to even get involved in this whole charade!'

Matias opened his mouth to dismiss her snide but perfectly understandable interruption. Instead he found himself saying, *sotto voce*, and with a sincerity that cut right through all his usual weary cynicism, 'I've lost touch with my mother over the years. Taken care of the essentials and visited only as a matter of duty. Time has wreaked destruction over the years…and my values are so different from my parents'… *Hell*.' He raked his fingers through his hair and flushed darkly, for once caught on the back foot. 'Reconnecting with her, even in these utterly fake circumstances, isn't something I'm plotting to destroy before it's even really begun.'

'Matias…'

'I'll see you tomorrow.'

The conversation was closed. She could see it in his shuttered expression and hear it in the finality of his voice. He'd opened up and already he was regretting it. She was filled with such an intense craving for this moment of shared confidence to be prolonged that it terrified her.

'I'll make sure a guest room is prepared for you,' she muttered—a reminder more to herself than anyone else of the boundary lines within this little game of theirs.

He returned a clipped nod.

Being out of his suffocating company for a handful of hours should have come as blessed relief, but instead Georgina spent the evening unable to concentrate on anything. She prepared one of the guest rooms for Matias, realising as she did so that she hadn't actually been into this particular bedroom since her parents had left. It was dusty and smelled airless.

She aired it all. and then had to fight down thoughts of Matias in the bed. How could these disturbing feelings still have lodgings inside her? Was it the oddness of their situation? Were there still embers of those flames that had been ignited all those years ago that had never been entirely doused? What had she unleashed with this ill-conceived plan of hers?

Following that thought through to any kind of conclusion made her quail with apprehension. So instead she sat at her desk and brought her computer to life, scrolling through the extensive archives of food photos that had inspired her in the past and making rough notes on what sort of vibe she wanted to get for her young chef.

But her mind was a million miles away. Things were no longer reassuringly black and white. There was an ocean of grey in between and she was realising that she was a very poor swimmer...

The following morning she chose her outfit carefully. Casual cotton, ankle-length khaki trousers and a simple white ribbed tee shirt which she tucked into the waistband of the trousers. The same sandals she had worn the day before. Cool, easy to wear clothes put together in a way that gave her shape, brought out the best in her. Clothes that afforded her some measure of the control which she felt she needed—because the minute she was with Matias, playing this stupid game, control seemed to slip through her fingers like water through the holes of a colander.

She heard the buzz of the doorbell and a surge of nerves washed over her, but she was as cool as a cucumber when she pulled open the door to see Matias, lounging against the doorframe, finger poised to ring again, even though she'd answered the door in seconds.

It was another brilliant day and he was in a white polo shirt and a pair of low-slung faded jeans that lovingly hugged the muscular length of his legs. Her eyes drifted helplessly to the dark hair on his forearms and the way that dark hair curled around the dull matt silver of his watch strap.

She dragged her eyes away and said abruptly, 'You don't have to do this. Rose would be none the wiser if you go to the next town and work to your heart's content and then return at a respectable hour for us to join her.'

'Strangely, I'm uncomfortable with such large-scale lying. Your one whopper is bad enough without adding to the tally by telling a few more lies. Now, let me in. I'd really like to see some of your work.'

He straightened, and after a few seconds' hesitation Georgina stood back.

He brushed past her into the hall. 'I haven't been here in a long time...'

He looked around him at a house that was homely and large but in need of some TLC. He could count the number of times he had stepped foot in this house on the fingers of one hand. For some reason gatherings had always been held by his parents. Or maybe he just hadn't been around for the ones that had taken place here.

'Why?' he asked with genuine curiosity.

Why do you continue to live here...? Why not spread your wings...? You're young and sexy...

The house was typically the residence of middle-aged people who had no real interest in décor. The wallpaper harked back to an era of flowers and birds and was faded. The wood was shiny, the rugs attractive but threadbare. Everything looked tired and old-fashioned. David and Alison White, from memory, both had the academic's typical disregard for their surroundings, and for the first time he could understand why their creative daughter had been so enchanted by his parents' flamboyance.

'Why what?'

Matias shrugged, letting it go. 'Where do you work?'

Georgina hesitated, then led him to the conservatory at the back, which she had converted into a studio. Her portfolio of work was neatly stacked on shelves and in a metal filing cabinet, and some of her photos hung on the wall. Her camera equipment was extensive.

Matias was seriously impressed. He peered at the photos on display, standing back and then examining them in detail while she described the ins and outs of food photography and what it entailed with some embarrassment.

Eventually her voice tapered off and she hovered, arms folded, by the door. 'You honestly don't have to say that you like them,' she blurted out.

'They're...amazing.'

He looked at her in silence for a few long seconds and she could feel her face getting hotter and hotter and redder and redder.

'Who are your clients?'

'Some chefs…obviously…' She spun round and began heading out of the conservatory. Having him look at her work had made her feel exposed and vulnerable for some reason, and the sooner they headed off the better. 'Usually up-and-coming ones, because I'm relatively cheap. Also I've made a name for myself in the restaurant trade around here. That's my bread and butter, really. There are always new dishes they want photographed. And I've had a couple of commissions from publishing houses for recipe books…'

She blathered on witlessly and followed him out to his car. His driver had clearly vanished back to London.

'So…' Matias switched on the engine and the powerful car roared into life, but he didn't drive off, instead choosing to lean against the door to look at her. 'A day doing what loved-up couples apparently do. My mother was up at the crack of dawn preparing a picnic for our trip to the seaside. Now, I may have lived here for years, but you'll have to provide directions. I can't tell you the last time I went to a beach down here.'

'Not even with one of those blondes you've sometimes brought down?' Georgina said, disobeying her own mantra about steering clear of anything remotely personal and reverting to the comfort zone of bickering ex-neighbours.

She briefly gave him a series of directions, but her curiosity about him had been unleashed and she was finding it hard to stuff it back into its box.

'I don't do beach trips with women,' Matias drawled, glancing at her sideways as he began driving away from the house. 'And I certainly don't do home-made picnics.'

'Why?'

'Because I like keeping it light.'

'Why?'

'You're very curious, aren't you?' Matias murmured. 'Do you find me as fascinating now as you did all those years ago?'

Georgina went beetroot-red. 'I don't know what you're talking about,' she said woodenly.

'No? I remember you used to follow me with your eyes…always curious about my life at boarding school…always taking pot-shots at the girls I sometimes brought home…'

'Polite,' Georgina corrected in a strangled voice. 'I was *polite* when I asked you about school. You were the only person I knew at a boarding school! And I didn't take pot-shots at those girls. I may have sniggered a bit because they were all so empty-headed, and gazed at you as though you were the next best thing to sliced bread, but it certainly wasn't because I found you *fascinating*.'

Matias shrugged, but a half-smile tugged the corners of his mouth.

Mortified, Georgina could barely appreciate the splendour of the beach when they finally got there, and although she made all the right noises about the hamper his mother had prepared she was barely able to think straight.

She'd been so careful all those years ago! She'd watched him from the side lines, safe in the certainty that her silly crush was something no one knew about—least of all him. She'd downplayed the jealousy she'd felt when, over the years, she had noted all the wafer-thin models who had hung like limpets on his arm, gazing up at him with adoring eyes. She'd told herself that she was far happier with her photography and a sense of direction in her life.

To know that he had seen through all that made her squirm with shame and embarrassment. Made her realise how sharp his instincts were when it came to the opposite sex. Made her see just how dangerous this little game could become if she allowed her eyes to stray. If he noticed… If he jumped to conclusions…

They'd hit the beach at peak time, but they managed to find themselves a relatively serene spot and he laid out the picnic with exaggerated ceremony. He'd shrugged off her random remark of earlier, and barely glanced at her now as they settled on the large rug his mother had packed along with the food.

'Hot,' Matias said, sprawling on the ground with his hands behind his head, staring up at a cloudless blue sky from behind his designer sunglasses. 'If I'd known it was going to be this hot I would have suggested we come equipped with our swimming gear—although swimming gear in these waters is strictly called a wetsuit. Unless you happen to be extremely hardy? Are you?'

'I've been swimming a few times,' Georgina said politely, gazing off into the distance but very much aware of his loose-limbed elegant body on the rug next to her. She was sitting up, as rigid as a plank of wood. He was sprawled on his back, his body language unspeakably relaxed and sexy.

'Very impressive.'

'You don't have to put on a show when it's just the two of us, Matias. I know the last thing you've ever been when it comes to me is *impressed*.'

'You need to lose your insecurities. Earlier I asked you a question.'

'What question?'

Since when was Matias Silva equipped to talk to her about insecurities? Who did he think he was?

He was looking at her. She could feel the weight of his gaze on her and it made her squirm.

'Why are you still working here? Living here? In your parents' house? I would have thought that after you were let down by that loser this would be the last place you would want to stay.'

Georgina turned to look at him for a few seconds, then looked away. The questions felt invasive, and way too personal. She'd barely talked to anyone in any depth about the break-up all those years ago. She'd just got on with her life and side-stepped the pity and the sympathy.

'There's a big, bad world out there,' he mused, ignoring every *No Entry* sign she was erecting and barging through. 'Maybe you've stayed here because, for all your talk about still being a fan of happy-ever-after fairy tales, it's safer for you to avoid putting it to the test and you can do that by burying yourself in your parents' house and daydreaming about a world of possibilities you have no intention of exploring.'

'This suits me at the moment.' She was holding on to her temper with difficulty, but she wanted to throw something hard and heavy at his beautiful head. 'I can save while I'm here. And, trust me, Matias, if something came up and made me think about leaving then I would.'

'Something like what?'

'I'm finished with this conversation!'

She sprang up and began walking fast in the direction of the car, not looking back to see whether he was following or not. He was making her confront deep-seated insecurities about the direction of her life and she loathed him for it.

Yes, of *course* she knew that there were more adventurous roads she could go down! But he didn't understand and he never would. He had blown off this village when he was a teenager and he had never looked back. He had left as one person and morphed into a completely different one. He had pursued wealth and power and now he thought the way wealthy, powerful people thought. In black and white.

She glanced behind her to see him sweeping up the picnic, hardly touched, and carelessly flinging everything inside the basket which had been provided.

'What I think…what I choose to do with my life… is none of your business!' She turned to him with furious eyes as soon as they were in the car and the engine was switched on.

'You're right.' Matias looked at her levelly—a long, unflinching look that she had difficulty returning. 'But do you want to know something?'

'No!'

'Well, I'll tell you anyway—considering you've made it your life's work to tell *me* what you think of *me* and *my* life choices. You're a coward. You talk the talk, but you don't walk the walk. You're in your parents' house because you're afraid of all the crap that happens out there in the big, bad world. You might have in your head some nonsense about the perfect man, but you won't be looking too hard for him because you don't want to get hurt again.'

'That's not true!'

Her huge green eyes held a mixture of hurt and defiance and Matias knew that he had put that look there. But she'd never been backward at coming forward, and if she couldn't stand the heat, then she had to get out of the kitchen.

'Did he hurt you that much, Georgie?'

'I *hate* you.'

'No, you don't.'

He smoothed his finger over her cheek and this time he let it linger there. And she couldn't push him away because she was mesmerised by his touch and by the *nearness* of him.

She leaned towards him, the palms of her hands flat on the smooth leather of the passenger seat. 'What do *you* think?' she muttered gruffly.

He cupped the side of her face with his hand. 'I think you were probably a lot less hurt than you should have been if you actually loved the guy, but you never loved him.'

'How would *you* know?'

'He was never the one for you,' Matias said gently. 'Which I said to you at the time. But your parents approved of him and that was enough for you to get sucked into something that never had legs in the first place.'

'You think you know it all!'

'I know enough.'

'You've never had a long-standing, successful relationship!'

'Never wanted one.'

'Because…?' Georgina looked at him with mutinous, challenging green eyes.

'Because I prefer to direct my energies into the more tangible business of making money.'

'Why the fixation with money?' Georgina dared to ask, even though his shuttered expression was directing her away from any more personal questions.

'It's not as though that was the sort of thing that ever mattered to your parents.'

He had eased out of the parking slot and they were steadily making their way back to his mother's house. She'd barely noticed because she'd been so wrapped up in him.

How could he be so full of contradictions? How could he be so charming, so lazily persuasive, so charismatic…and yet so coolly remote and untouchable?

'But that's just it,' Matias said, sliding icy grey eyes across at her. 'A bit of farming…a bit of hocuspocus herbalism…a spot of magic massage here and there… You can pull that off when you're buried deep in a village somewhere, but the real world is slightly more judgemental about that kind of nonsense. I found that out myself when I went to boarding school.'

'What do you mean?'

'I mean,' Matias gritted, his voice hard-edged and unforgiving, 'when you're thirteen and your parents are pulling up to collect you in a camper van and your mother is promising discounted Reiki sessions to the parents of boys you've only known for five minutes… Well, let's just say that's the stuff that learning curves are made from.'

'I never knew…' She only realised that the car had stopped when he killed the engine.

'No need for the tea and sympathy, Georgie. I got exactly what I wanted out of that school. I learnt what needed to be done to get me where I needed to get. Money, *darling*, may be the root of all evil in *your* critical, judgemental eyes, but it's also the greatest passport to freedom. Have enough of it and the world is yours for the taking.'

He opened his door and she scrambled out too, protesting heatedly that the last thing she was, was *judgemental* and fighting off a tug of sympathy for that young boy stuck in a boarding school where he didn't fit in.

She was all hot and bothered, with eyes only for the man striding ahead of her towards the front door.

'Not the right time,' Matias cautioned, barely breaking stride.

'What are you talking about?'

'An angry, ranting girlfriend? What will my mother think?'

He looked down at her. Her colourful hair was everywhere, her bright green eyes were flashing fire, her full mouth was half open. She was the very picture of passion. She was the most tempting creature he had ever seen and he was shocked at how powerful the urge to take her suddenly was.

He drew his breath in sharply, hearing the sound of his mother's footsteps. And then the door opened, and Matias lowered his head and did what he'd wanted to do all day.

He kissed Georgie.

No messing about with anything delicate or gentle or tentative. This was a real kiss, hot and hard and hungry, his tongue probing, meshing with hers.

His erection was rock-hard, throbbing. Her softness was a powerful aphrodisiac and the swell of her generous breasts so close to his chest set up a series of graphic sexual images in his head.

'You two should get a room!'

His mother's voice was amused and warm and it broke the spell. Matias pulled back, raked his fingers through his hair, and realised that he couldn't remember when he had last lost control like that.

CHAPTER FIVE

HOT RED COLOUR surged up into Georgina's cheeks. She sprang back as though she'd been burnt. She couldn't meet Rose's eyes, nor could she risk looking at Matias, so she stared down at the ground instead, wishing it could swallow her up.

'Well done,' Matias murmured.

He urged her into the house, following his mother, who was disappearing off to the sitting room and chatting animatedly and thinking… Heaven only knew what, Georgina worried. Certainly not that these were two people due to break up in under two weeks.

'What are you talking about?'

Still reeling, Georgina stopped dead in her tracks and looked up at him. Ahead, Rose was peppering them with questions about their day, heading for her favourite chair. Georgina cringed at the thought of having to reproduce excited tales of how their day had gone.

'I think we've managed to convince my mother that everything's on track between us. She couldn't have looked happier when she saw me kiss you.' He paused. 'Award-winning performance, Georgie,' he said roughly.

He glanced away for a few seconds, during which time her mind went completely blank before it cranked back into gear and joined up the dots.

What she'd seen as devastating had been a routine, necessary pretend show of affection for him. He hadn't wanted his mother to open the door to a scowling girlfriend in the throes of a heated argument with her son so he had kissed her to shut her up.

It had worked.

The only problem was that she had returned the kiss as though it had been the real thing. She had thrown herself into it body and soul, never wanting it to end. That kiss had flung open a door to feelings she now shamefully realised were still very much alive and kicking.

Humiliation stiffened her backbone and she clenched her jaw and took a few deep breaths before answering. 'Thanks. Wouldn't have done for your mother to have seen us bickering.'

'When you returned that kiss I almost got the impression that it was more than just a response to keep this charade on the right track...'

Georgina laughed. It sounded brittle to her ears but pride had kicked in. This wasn't real life. This was make-believe. To him she was still the annoying girl next door, and just because she'd had a make-over it didn't mean that she'd suddenly turned into

Cinderella…it didn't mean that Prince Charming was going to be falling head over heels in love with her.

She met his eyes and wished that she could see what he was thinking. But his expression was shuttered. Was he desperately trying to contain his impatience? His apprehension that she'd been a little too enthusiastic? Was he terrified that he might have to start erecting *No Trespass* signs around himself to keep her at bay?

Her mouth was still tingling from the feel of his tongue meshing so erotically with hers. She wanted to touch her lips with her fingers to cool them, and just in case she did that unthinkingly she clenched her fists at her sides.

'Don't be crazy,' she said gruffly. 'Why would you get that idea? I keep telling you that you're not my type…'

'Ever thought that you might be attracted physically to a guy who *isn't* your type?'

'No. I like to believe that I approach relationships with my head and not my body. Especially after the business with Robbie—which you've made sure to remind me was the biggest mistake a girl could ever have made.'

'I was under the impression that he was definitely an *approach with your head* situation…'

Georgina flushed and fidgeted.

Matias shifted uncomfortably and raked his fingers through his hair. He stared down at her, his body rigid with tension.

'You don't have to worry that I'm going to throw myself at you, Matias,' Georgina said impatiently—because how much more obvious could a person make it that he was worried she might start making a play for him?

'What makes you think I would be worried if you threw yourself at me?'

Thick silence settled between them. Georgina had no idea what he was trying to say. Was he actually *flirting* with her?

She stared at him, open-mouthed, and he brushed his finger along her lower lip. Conflicting sensations flooded through her. Shock…unbearable excitement… shameful arousal…and absolute fear. Because this was definitely unknown and unexpected territory.

He didn't take his finger away. Instead he stepped towards her and cupped the side of her face with his hand.

'I don't know…what you're trying to say…' she stammered, for want of anything better.

'Liar. You know *exactly* what I'm trying to say.'

Matias smiled slowly. He took his time. He leaned in to her. It was an easy, slow movement that paralysed her to the spot. This time he kissed her gently and tenderly, and she couldn't stop a sigh of forbidden pleasure as she leaned up and closed her eyes and kissed him back. Because she was lost and she couldn't help herself.

Her arms were doing just what she'd hoped they

wouldn't do—winding round his neck and drawing him towards her. Her breasts were squashed against his chest as they unconsciously closed the gap between themselves, and she could feel the scratchy tingle of her nipples against her bra.

She wanted him to touch her so badly that it was a physical ache. And *she* wanted to touch *him*. More than anything else in the world she wanted to take his bigness between her hands and *feel* him.

The craving inside her was so intense that it took her breath away. It terrified her.

She had no idea what was happening because she had never felt anything so powerful in her life before. It carried the force of a tsunami, and some primitive instinct told her that it was a force she had to keep at bay or beware the consequences.

With a gasp, she pushed him away. He immediately stepped back, although he continued to stare down at her, his beautiful eyes unfathomable.

'This isn't part of the deal,' she hissed fiercely.

She wrapped her arms around her body and met his stare head-on. She wondered if he thought he was so irresistible that she just wouldn't be able to help but melt into his arms like a Victorian maiden.

'This is an…an…*arrangement*… And if I remember correctly it's an arrangement *you* rejected until you decided that you had no option but to accept because you couldn't face letting your mother down. This isn't *real*. Fantasy isn't going to get in the way of *reality*.'

'But that's not what this is about, is it?' Matias purred, infuriatingly calm.

'Then what was…what was…*that*…?'

'You mean our passionate kiss?'

Georgina glowered, her colour high, her whole body aflame with a longing she couldn't quite manage to douse.

'Lust,' Matias murmured succinctly.

One word but it couldn't have been more erotic or more devastating. Because it was stripped of all the pretty packaging that he might have used to soften its naked potency.

'I don't get it,' he continued in a low, lazy, wildly sensual voice, 'but I want you.'

'No,' Georgina whispered, 'you don't. I get on your nerves! How many times have you told me that? You and I have *nothing* in common! We're like chalk and cheese! And don't even *think* about telling me that opposites attract, because we're not just opposites…we're so different we could have come from different planets!'

'Mysterious, isn't it?'

'Is that all you have to say?'

'I'm being honest.' He shrugged. 'So what if we're from different planets? What does that have to do with whether we want to find the nearest bed…or table…or sofa…or patch of ground…and rip one another's clothes off? This isn't about confusing reality with fantasy, Georgie. This isn't about us actually *having* a relationship. No, this is way more elemental than that. I see you and I want to taste you.'

'Matias…*stop*!'

'Why? Am I turning you on?'

'No! I don't want you! You're mistaken!' Georgina heard the pathetic desperation in her voice with dismay. 'Your mother is waiting for us! I… She's going to come out in a minute… She's going to want to know what's going on…'

'She won't come out,' Matias assured her in a deep, velvety voice that was just ever so slightly amused. 'She's leaving the love birds to have fun together without her getting in the way. Why do you think she propelled us off for a session at the beach? Why do you think she insisted on us being together under the same roof while we're here?'

'Well, she won't find us doing anything together! That kiss? It never happened!'

'No?' he drawled, eyebrows raised. 'Why's that?'

'Because I'm not *you*, Matias.' She was relieved that she had regained control over her vocal cords. She wanted to sound cool and dismissive and she wasn't too far away from succeeding. Logic and common sense might have flown through the window for a few seconds, but both were back now. 'I don't do passing-ships-in-the-night relationships.'

'Have you ever tried?'

'I don't need to. I know that kind of thing is not for me.'

'So instead you make a checklist for the perfect guy and see if reality tallies up with the picture you've got in your head?'

'There's nothing wrong with knowing what you want when it comes to finding a partner.'

'And tell me how that worked for you last time round, Georgie. Tell me how that's been working for you since.'

'That's not fair.'

'I know,' Matias said roughly. 'I apologise. But sometimes you have to jettison the checklist and take what you want.'

'Not me. Robbie wasn't right. I know I got seduced by the fact that my parents approved, and they'd never really approved of any of the boyfriends I'd ever brought back home, And I know that since Robbie I've had a break from men…who wouldn't? but it doesn't mean that I have to do something just because…because…'

'Because it feels good?'

He shrugged and stepped away from her, and suddenly the air between them felt cool, the void too gaping for comfort. She wanted him back, closer to her, and she fought the impulse to step towards him.

'Just because something feels good it doesn't mean that you have to reach out and take it. I'm not a kid in a sweet shop with permission to grab whatever candy takes my fancy before I get bored with the game and move on.'

'So serious…' Matias said, heading towards the sitting room, leaving Georgina to traipse along in his wake. 'So intent on passing up on the fun elements of life.'

Georgina heard the lazy amusement in his voice and realised that he didn't really care one way or another whether she took him up on his offer or not.

He was attracted to her, and he'd probably picked up similar vibes from her. She could try and argue that he was off target but why waste her time doing that? The man had vast experience when it came to women and he would burst out laughing if she tried to pretend that she didn't find him attractive.

But sleep with him?

No way!

'I am *not* passing up on the fun elements of life just because I've turned you down!' She yanked him to a stop so that she could glare up at him. 'Matias, you…you're the most egotistical man I have ever met in my entire life!'

'Okay.'

'*Okay?* Is that all you have to say?'

'What more do you want me to add to the mix, Georgie?'

'You have *never* been attracted to me in your life before,' she snapped, hands on her hips, one eye on the sitting room door, which was slightly ajar, making sure to keep her voice low because she knew walls had ears.

Matias looked at her, his head tilted to one side in thoughtful contemplation. 'Because you've always taken such pains to be irritating, Georgie. Always on a soap box…always dressed like a hippy with a cause. Why have you never made the most of your looks?'

'How *dare* you…?'

'You opened this conversation. Don't start trying to shut it down because you don't like the direction it's taking. You're sexy as hell, but this is the first time I've ever noticed because you've always kept your voluptuous curves hidden away.'

Sexy as hell? Voluptuous curves? The man was so shallow, Georgina thought weakly. But something inside her was twisting and melting. Her body was letting her down badly, responding to his superficial compliments as though they really mattered.

'You really just have one thing in mind when you look at a woman, don't you?' she threw at him.

He didn't look unduly bothered. 'We could keep going round in circles for ever on this one, Georgie.'

He took her arm and she bristled at his touch, as though she'd been plugged into an electrical socket.

'But, much as my mother is keen on giving us some downtime together, there's only so long she will hang on before curiosity kicks in and she comes out to make sure we haven't dropped dead in the hallway.'

Which left the conversation in mid-air. He'd started something that she somehow hadn't managed to finish, even though she'd tried. She'd made a big deal of telling him that she wasn't interested in any sort of casual sexual relationship with him that would never go anywhere, but she hadn't ended up feeling victorious or satisfied with the stance she had taken.

* * *

Georgina spent the remainder of the evening in a state of restless flux. She felt as though she'd been put into a washing machine with the cycle turned to spin. All her preconceived notions about Matias had taken a beating, and so had her precious principles about what made sense when it came to relationships.

He'd come along, a devil in disguise, and she couldn't stop her mind from playing over and over what he had said to her.

His casual touches over the course of the evening burned through her clothing and made her shiver. The deep, sexy timbre of his voice sent chills racing up and down her spin. The proud angle of his head and the startling beauty of his lean face made her shiver and think forbidden thoughts.

And soon they would be leaving together. He would be spending the night in her house. In a different room, but still… The thought of them being alone together after what he had said, with the atmosphere so charged between them, brought her out in a cold sweat.

The conversation drifted around her. She participated, but her voice seemed to come from a long way away, barely penetrating the chaos of her thoughts, which were all over the place.

She surfaced to hear Rose asking her about the upcoming shoot.

'How will those pictures of my carrots and asparagus come out, do you think?' She was smiling at Matias. 'You wouldn't believe how talented she is,' she confided proudly. 'And always doing her best to promote the produce here.'

'I saw some samples of her work.' His silver-grey eyes settled on Georgina, bringing a pink tinge to her cheeks. 'She's brilliant.'

The pink tinge turned to a deep red—a mixture of pleasure and embarrassment at the flattery. She launched into a jerky speech about the chef who had commissioned her for the photo shoot, and heard herself babbling on about the procedure for getting just the right shots put together so that everything looked natural, but enhanced.

'Anyway,' she concluded, wanting to feel more relieved than she actually did at the thought of having a perfectly valid excuse not to spend the next day with Matias, even if the night ahead lay before her like the threat of the hangman's noose, 'the shoot is tomorrow and then I shall be going to her place in the evening to show her the mark-ups, get her opinions. So...'

She turned to Matias with a phoney smile and he raised both eyebrows, unfazed.

'It'll be a perfect opportunity for you to catch up on all that...er...work you told me you had to do...' she said, and turned to Rose with a woman-to-woman look. 'He's a workaholic... Sometimes I have to drag him away from that computer of his! I shall have to change that or we'll soon find ourselves at loggerheads! That's just the sort of thing that can bring a relationship crashing down. You know how women *love* attention…and a man whose first love is his work…? Well…'

Rose looked at her thoughtfully. 'You could take Matias with you in the evening. I'm sure Melissa wouldn't mind meeting your boyfriend, Georgie, and Matias…? Georgie's right. Relationships are all about compromise. It would do you good to see her in action…'

'But it's going to be baking hot,' Georgina protested, hanging on to her smile by a thread. 'And she lives up a hill! I usually walk up for the exercise! But Matias…' She looked over to him and said, with complete honesty, 'He doesn't do walking…'

'I could start,' Matias returned without batting an eye. 'How steep can a hill be around here? I might not tackle Everest, but I'm as fit as the next man, my darling—as well you know.'

Rose looked delighted. Matias looked highly amused. And Georgina… She felt the pit of her stomach fall away, even though she knew that she was being silly.

Matias wasn't going to chase her like a horny teenager pursuing a hot prom queen. He could have any woman on the planet he wanted. And if he wanted her for a couple of seconds because they'd been thrown together, because he was bored and between women and she happened to be wearing less hippy-like clothes, then the feeling wouldn't last.

* * *

'Nice try.' It was the first thing he said on their way to her house. 'I'm a workaholic you're going to come to blows with sooner rather than later because you want romance and I'm too busy staring at my computer to indulge you…'

The night air was humid and still. Georgina was keeping her distance but she could still feel his powerful personality wrapping itself around her, wanting to draw her close.

'It's true. You are a workaholic… I'm not breaking new ground by pointing out the obvious.'

'But there was just a whiff of desperation when you started clutching at that straw…and in your eagerness to make sure I'm not around tomorrow. Are you nervous at the prospect of the both of us in the same house?'

'No! I told you that I don't believe in…in…'

She eyed her house with relief. They had chosen to walk there rather than take the car and it beckoned to her like a port in a storm—because once inside she could flee to her room and shove him into the guest room she had prepared.

'Casual, scintillating sex? Don't worry. I won't come knocking on your door in the middle of the night…'

Which immediately conjured up all the wrong images in her head.

'And I'll leave you alone during the day too, to do what you have to do, because as it happens you're right. I have a lot of work to get through. I shall take myself off to a business in Padstow I've been contemplating buying for the past couple of months. So you can relax. Reluctance in a woman has always been a turn-off for me.'

They'd reached the house and he lounged against the door as she unlocked it and then preceded him into the hallway. When he paused she reluctantly turned and looked at him.

His dark eyes were cool. 'I'll be ready at six for this walk I shouldn't be able to do because the only exercise I'm capable of is getting into the back seat of my chauffeur-driven car.'

'Matias…'

'Goodnight, Georgie. Sleep well in your empty bed.'

With which he vanished in the direction of her father's office at the other end of the house, leaving her to pointlessly mull over the joyless coldness of her empty bed and to spend the night tossing and turning, wondering where he was in the house and whether he was thinking about her at all, before finally falling into a restless sleep at a little after midnight.

She barely looked up from her work the following day. True to his word, Matias had disappeared, but his absence—perversely—did nothing to quell the tumult of her thoughts, and she was keyed up when, at a little after six, he appeared in the doorway of her studio without warning.

She was ready to go and had done away with any girly dress code. There was too much heavy humidity in the air, and the strenuous walk up to Melissa's house would be impossible in something frothy and frivolous.

He, likewise, was in practical gear. Faded jeans, a dark grey short-sleeved polo shirt and walking boots. For a few seconds she lost herself in just looking at him, because he was drop-dead gorgeous, but then she gathered herself and began collecting everything she had to take with her, stuffing tablet, portfolio and camera in a weatherproof rucksack which he promptly took from her.

'I'll carry it,' he said smoothly. 'I'm stronger than I look.'

He grinned and she reluctantly smiled back, relieved that a truce appeared to have been called. She'd spent a lifetime bickering with him, so how was it that she now felt at odds with herself, unable to function properly, at the thought of him withdrawing from her?

He obediently followed her to her old car, and immediately turned to her once he was inside. 'Tell me about your friend Melissa.'

The sexy teasing was gone, replaced by a genuinely friendly interest—and Georgina hated it. A Pandora's box had been opened but now everything was changing back. How was she going to deal with it? She missed the way those dark, lazy eyes had made her feel like a woman. She missed the way his husky drawl had made her melt and feel restless, as though there was an itch deep inside her that needed to be scratched.

She asked him about his day, returning polite interest with polite interest, but once they'd parked the car and begun trekking up the hill to Melissa's house conversation flagged because it was just too unbearably hot and still to talk.

For once, Georgina felt too puffed to appreciate the undisturbed countryside around her. The winding trek up was usually something to be done slowly, but this time she was relieved when it was over—when the front door was opened and the cool of the house greeted them.

Melissa suited her surroundings. It was something Georgina clearly scarcely registered, but as introductions were made Matias was startled to realise that as little as two months ago he would have had no time for the chef's wildly eccentric dress code. It would have been a little too reminiscent of what he had grown up with, and what he associated with the sort of carefree irresponsibility that never got anyone anywhere.

Now he had to concede that a lot had changed on that front. He'd switched off from the small details of his mother's life, accepting the limitations between them as just the way it was. The further he'd travelled away from his past, the greater the chasm between them had grown. He didn't know when that journey away from his parents had begun. He just knew that it was a journey from which there had been no turning back.

That was life.

Until now, when everything he'd learned to accept had been turned on its head. He and his mother were daily groping their way towards a deeper connection, and that involved him hearing the ins and outs of her life—the small things he had missed from the bigger picture. He could understand now how and why Georgina had taken it upon herself to tell the little lie that had led them to the place they were now, and he wasn't sorry about any of it.

Caught up in the business of cropping images and discussing final layouts, Georgina only noticed the passing of time when Matias appeared in the doorway to the kitchen.

'I think you two might want to come out here and have a look,' he said.

Georgina looked up and blinked. It took her a few seconds to register, but she didn't have to go out to see what was happening and neither did Melissa. They were both accustomed to the swift weather changes in this part of the world and she looked at her friend with dismay.

'I knew it!' Melissa stood up, stretched, and gathered up her long brown hair into an unruly ponytail. 'I spoke to my brother on the phone this afternoon and I *told* him that it was getting way too hot and way too humid for comfort!' She laughed and began moving towards the kitchen door. 'Stay put, you two. I'm going to head upstairs and make sure that all the windows in the house are shut!'

'Melissa…' Georgina sprang upright. 'We need to get going…'

There was the sudden whiteness of lightning and then, a few seconds later, a crack of thunder loud enough to make her jump. She moved to where Matias was hurriedly shutting the kitchen door and closing the window against the pounding of rain that was as sudden as it was fierce.

She raced to the window and peered out. The rain was a sheet of water driving across the horizon. The sky, which had been so bright and blue for weeks, was an angry black. The wind was gathering momentum and howling. There was no way they were going to be able to walk back down that hill to her car.

'There's no point worrying about the weather,' Matias said from behind her.

Their eyes met, reflected in the window pane with the stormy evening an unfolding drama outside. A frisson of apprehension rippled through her and for a few fraught seconds she couldn't break the connection as they both stared at one another in the glass pane.

'Matias, you don't understand…' She edged away, got past him, and then turned round to look at him.

'So it's raining?' He shrugged. 'I'd forgotten how fast this kind of thing happens down here.'

'This is a disaster…' Her voice was barely audible over the pounding of the rain on the roof and against the windows.

Flash flooding.

Matias might stand there looking as though he didn't have a care in the world, but he never came to Cornwall and, despite what he'd just said, he wouldn't remember how brutal these downpours could become. He lived his charmed life in the city, where the weather was a lot more polite.

'You need to revisit your definition of disaster.' Matias dumped his glass in the sink and then turned to her, leaning against the counter just as the kitchen door flew open and Melissa made a dramatic entrance.

'Windows all shut!' she cried gaily, with the joyful satisfaction of someone announcing the winning raffle ticket number. 'I've never seen anything like this before! I should have guessed, though! The heat we've been having over the last couple of weeks… Well, everyone's been saying we're due for a storm!'

'"Storm" is a bit of an understatement, isn't it, Melissa?' Georgina smiled weakly and followed her friend to the fridge, to give her hand getting stuff out for a meal.

'It's wild out there!' Melissa peered past Georgina to where Matias was still lounging against the counter. 'But no matter!' She winked at him. 'You city gents need to experience a little of what this part of the world is all about! Now, scoot—both of you! I shall fix you a gourmet meal and then you can get cosy in the bedroom I've prepared!'

CHAPTER SIX

BEDROOM I'VE PREPARED...

They were supposed to be an item. There was no way Georgina could express to her friend the horror she felt at the prospect of sharing a room with Matias. What young couple, going out with one another, slept in separate bedrooms? Like survivors from the Victorian age?

Melissa would burst out laughing, would think that Georgina was having her on. They lived in a village. How long would it be before gossip did the rounds and someone told someone who told someone else that the 'loved-up' couple were as distant as two strangers?

It was a risk that Georgina was not willing to take—not now that they were in the thick of this ill-thought-out charade.

She could barely enjoy the fabulous meal Melissa had prepared. She heard herself making all the expected appreciative noises at the ingredients that had been used in its preparation—ingredients provided by Rose, produce from her farm.

She knew that Matias was laying on the charm. For all his ruthlessness, his indifference when it came to emotions and his coldness, he could be persuasive, and by the end of the evening, with the rain still slamming against the window panes and no hope at all of risking any kind of trek back down the hill to the car, Melissa had joined his fan club.

'He's brilliant,' she whispered, tugging Georgina back while Matias preceded them up the stairs. 'Honestly, Georgie, I was beginning to despair that you would ever move on after that creep.'

'Brilliant?' Georgina asked weakly. 'He should be the last person you think is *brilliant*.' She laughed to dilute the urgency of what she was saying. 'He's the least laid-back, least relaxed person in the world! He's a workaholic who has no time for much except the business of making money.'

'I know!' Melissa smiled. 'And I love that he doesn't try and gloss over that fact. Honesty in a guy is so refreshing. And besides, aren't we both workaholics in our own way?'

'What do you mean?'

Brilliant? Refreshing? Honest? Suddenly Matias appeared to have attained all the attributes of a saint in waiting.

'Well, I don't know about you,' Melissa said wryly, 'but try tearing me away from the kitchen! Charlie says that I never have time to go to the movies or have days out because I'm always desperate to try some new idea for a dish! Now, if that's not being a workaholic, then what is? And I know you can be a slave to your camera. How many times have you told me that you've spent a Saturday looking at photos and working?'

'That's different,' Georgina said uncomfortably.

'No, it's not. It's fantastic that you've met your soul mate. I can tell there's a real connection there.'

They'd reached the spare bedroom and Melissa pushed open the door, and Georgina knew in that instant what it felt like to have tunnel vision because all she could see was the double bed.

'I know you love your space…' Georgina turned to Matias, who looked right back at her without revealing anything at all '…I'm sure Melissa won't mind if you want to sleep here on your own. I mean, this bed is really tiny—barely any room for two people to share. Matias likes his space…' She looked at her friend without actually meeting her warm brown eyes, realising, not for the first time, how hard deception could be. 'Don't you? Darling?' She turned to Melissa. 'He's a restless sleeper. Thrashes around.'

Share a bed? Inconceivable. Especially when the atmosphere between them was so…so alive with tension. No way!

'And *you* snore,' he said. 'You don't see *me* complaining.'

'I love it!' Melissa was looking between the two of them with bright-eyed interest and delight. 'I love it that you two are just so comfortable with one another.'

'I wouldn't dream of putting our host out,' Matias said smoothly, nailing the conversation dead.

He strolled towards Georgina and slung his arm over her shoulders. The warm weight of him stirred the melting pot of confusing reactions over which Georgina seemed to have no control. She could feel his skin burning into hers, insistent on making its effect felt.

'I've popped a couple of towels on the bed,' Melissa was saying, moving into the room and doing her best tour guide impression. 'There's lots of hot water—and, Georgie, I know we're not the same size, but I've put a tee shirt in the bathroom and you can use that if you want to…'

Georgina blanched. Matias had moved off to peer out of the window, where the rain continued to launch itself against the panes like bullets.

Her brain was beginning to malfunction. She couldn't take on board any further nightmares. The fact that Matias was as cool as a cucumber enraged her. Did he think that this was somehow going to play into his hands? No, of course he didn't, she told herself, because he would never pursue a reluctant woman—far less one who had shot him down in flames.

The door shut behind Melissa, and as soon as it had Georgina folded her arms and looked at him with undisguised horror. In return, he didn't look in the slightest bit concerned. He wasn't uncomfortable with the situation at all.

'Forget it,' he drawled as he began the process of undressing without so much as a by-your-leave.

'Forget what?' Georgina said tightly. The closer he was, the faster her pulses raced and the higher her colour became.

'Playing the outraged virgin. I didn't conspire to change the weather and your friend is simply being considerate in offering us a room for the night. I've phoned my mother and told her the situation.'

'I didn't see you do that!'

'That's because you were too busy dreading the prospect of sharing a bedroom with me.'

The buttons of his shirt were undone and her hungry eyes were inexorably drawn to the sliver of hard brown chest. Her pulses raced faster. She felt that in a minute she would forget how to breathe.

'Why do you think that is?' Matias murmured conversationally. 'Do you think you can't trust me not to try something because I've told you I fancy you? Didn't you believe me when I told you that I'm not into begging a woman to share my bed?'

Georgina croaked something. She knew what she wanted to say, and the person she wanted to be, but what emerged was nothing like what she had in mind. She wasn't controlled or cool or together. She was a nervous wreck and her body language was saying it all.

'Of course I believed you. That's not what this is about!'

'Maybe you don't trust yourself. Is that it, Georgie? Do you think that if you're too close to me you're not going to be able to help yourself?'

'I don't think I've ever heard anything so egotistical in my life before!'

'But then that's me, isn't it?' Matias told her, his voice cooling and his eyes hardening. 'An egotistical swine. No matter what I say or do, that will *always* be me, won't it?'

Somehow that level self-criticism felt like a slap in the face and Georgina knew that it wasn't true. Maybe once upon a time she had had those preconceived notions about him, but things had changed. He wasn't one-dimensional, he wasn't the cardboard cut-out of a callous son who never visited his poor mother and was only interested in making money.

She had seen the way he interacted with Rose and had glimpsed the vulnerable man beneath the cool mask. He had made her laugh with his quick wit and his sense of humour and had floored her with his intelligence and the breadth of his knowledge.

When she wasn't spoiling for a fight with him he got under her skin and opened her eyes to the man she'd always known existed, deep down. The man who still had the power to enthral her. And then there was his sizzling sex appeal, like nothing she had ever experienced… The last thing he was, was the arrogant egotist she had described him as being.

Honesty compelled her to say, 'You're not that.'

Matias shot her a surprised look and stilled. 'Meaning…?'

'I thought you were one thing,' she told him awkwardly, looking away and licking her lips nervously, but determined that he must know what she really thought. 'I thought you were cold and heartless for not coming down here more often. I thought you were just another arrogant guy wrapped up in making money and being rich, without any depth, but you're not. I can see the way you are with Rose...'

She reddened and stumbled over her words. She felt a bit as if she had thrown herself down a hole without knowing how far she would have to fall, and right now this meandering conversation made her feel that she was falling without a safety net.

'How's that?' Matias questioned gruffly.

'You do small things for her...reach for her if you think she needs help getting to her feet. You're solicitous. I think you feel you're really getting close to her and that you want to try and bridge whatever gap is there between you. Someone arrogant and selfish wouldn't care about bridging gaps.'

Georgina wondered whether she had said too much. His face was cool and remote. It was impossible to gauge what he was thinking.

'And I've seen the way you look around the house, looking for anything that might need replacing, keeping on top of things without Rose even really realising what you're doing. So, no. You're not an egotistical swine. Although...'

'Although...?'

'Although,' she said, bringing herself back on

point, 'you're still really full of yourself. And if we're sharing this bedroom then you keep to your side of the bed!'

She folded her arms and tilted her chin.

Matias laughed softly and then disappeared into the bathroom.

No change of clothes—nothing. Georgina eyed the tee shirt Melissa had left for her, and for good measure the pyjama shorts in soft cotton. Both were made for a size eight slightly built woman, but in the absence of anything else they would have to do.

She had no idea how long Matias was going to take, but somehow the thought of following behind him and showering in the shower he had just used made her skin tingle.

She tiptoed out of the bedroom and two doors down found the family bathroom. The cottage was small, but wonderfully equipped and eclectic, but Georgina was in far too much of a rush to admire the mosaic tiles, or the ornate gilt mirror over the old-fashioned sink, or the claw-footed bathtub.

Melissa would be downstairs, experimenting with food. Georgina knew that her friend was a night bird. But she took a very quick shower and was back in the bedroom before Matias was done. Who said that women took their time when it came to their ablutions?

The tee shirt was stretched tightly across her breasts but she had forgone the shorts, which hadn't fitted at all.

She huddled under the quilt on her side, all lights

in the room off, her eyes squeezed tightly shut. Her heart almost stopped beating when she heard the bathroom door open and then the soft footsteps of Matias before he slipped under the duvet next to her. The room was in darkness and the torrential rain, still banging against the window panes like angry fists, was strangely cosy and romantic.

She expected him to say something—something sarcastic or teasing or irritating. *Something*. He didn't.

He rolled onto his side, depressing the mattress with his weight. It made her cling further to her side, like a drowning man clinging to a lifebelt. His silence was oppressive. It made her wonder whether he was asleep. She found herself listening to his breathing and was then conscious of her own...

Georgina didn't know quite when she fell asleep, but she did know when she woke up.

The room was still pitch-black and for a short while she was utterly disorientated. The driving force of the rain had softened to a persistent patter, going from sounding like rocks against the windows to pebbles. She needed the toilet, and she cursed under her breath as she tiptoed her way through the bedroom, groping and taking her time because she didn't want to switch any lights on.

She couldn't have tried harder to be quiet, but the flush of the toilet and the sound of running water as she washed her hands resounded like the booming of church bells on a Sunday morning.

Tense as a bowstring, she crept stealthily towards the bed. Intent on making no noise, her narrowed eyes pinned to the inert dark shape on the bed, she took her eye off the ball. While her eyes were as keen as an eagle's, and her breathing as silent as a sigh, her feet were not quite so obliging.

An errant item of clothing on the ground was her downfall and she stumbled, panicked, reached out and fell with a crash.

She had a second's worth of mindless dismay and then Matias was there. He'd leapt from the bed, slammed on the lights and was kneeling on the ground before she had time to screech that she was perfectly fine.

Mortified, Georgina could barely look at him.

'What's going on?'

'Nothing! Nothing's going on.' She tried to scramble to her feet and winced in discomfort. 'I went to use the bathroom. I'm sorry I woke you up but it was dark and I didn't want to switch the light on.'

'Let me have a look.'

'Go away! Go back to sleep!'

'Don't be an idiot, Georgie.'

Georgina didn't answer. She was miserably conscious of her state of undress and the wretched many-sizes-too-small tee shirt which Melissa had kindly lent her. Not to mention the fact that she was in her underwear because she hadn't been able to squeeze herself into the insanely tiny pyjama shorts. She was aware of her legs on show, her thighs and her breasts,

which were bursting out of their over-tight confine-
ment. She was conscious of her body in a way she
had never been in her life before.

She jumped up—and subsided just as fast with a
little yelp of pain.

She abandoned the struggle as Matias scooped
her up in one fluid movement and carried her to the
bed, depositing her as carefully as if she were made
of china. He was thoughtful enough to switch off
the glaring overhead light, but then he immediately
switched on the lamp by the bed, which at least had
the benefit of being more forgiving.

Georgina kept her eyes tightly shut. Matias exam-
ined her foot, gently turning it in his hand, pressing
here and there and asking questions that she could
barely answer because her mouth was so dry.

'You'll live,' he said drily, straightening, at which
point Georgina risked looking at him.

He was wearing a pair of boxers and nothing else.
He was so beautiful that she felt faint. Her heart was
hammering and she knew that he would be able to
suss out perfectly well what it was she was trying
so hard not to convey—because there was a watchful stillness about him, an electric awareness of the
situation and only a tenuous thread tethering them
both to the straight and narrow.

He broke the connection, turned around.

'Matias…' She heard the hitch in her voice. 'What?'
He slowly swivelled to look at her, a taut, towering,
brooding presence that was all shadows and angles.

'Nothing…'

'Nothing? *Nothing?* In that case I'll go downstairs and work,' he said, not looking at her. 'That way you can sleep in peace and you won't have to try and creep around like a thief if you need to use the toilet.'

He began dressing, and for a few seconds Georgina watched him in tense silence, safely tucked under the duvet, legs drawn up to her chin.

Maybe I don't want you to go downstairs to work…maybe I don't want to sleep in peace…maybe I can't sleep in peace or do anything in peace with you around…maybe, just maybe, I'm sick to death of fighting this thing between us because, for me, it's been there for ever…

Never had she longed so much to say the unthinkable, to risk it all by throwing herself at him. She'd never had time for lust—but, then again, she'd never known what it felt like to be tempted.

Hands balled into fists, she bit down hard on the temptation and remained silent.

He didn't stick around. He got dressed fast and walked out of the room without a backward glance, and when the door was shut Georgina sagged back against the pillows and closed her eyes.

Her mobile phone was telling her that it was still very early in the morning. The sounds outside were reminding her of what awaited when dawn broke—water everywhere and rain turning the landscape into a miserable, sodden grey lake.

She was here.

He was here.

He'd never beg her. Or pursue her. Or even hint. He didn't care about her even if he did have a different take on her now that they'd been flung into one another's company, just as she had a different take on him.

She was a novelty for him. They weren't even *suited*! Could there be any *more* reasons for not doing what she was about to do…?

Her feet began taking her out of the bedroom and down the stairs. Her body was all for it. Her brain was on the back foot and no longer raising any objections. Having ruled the roost for so many years, it was now resigned to obeying stronger commands.

She knew the house and knew where he would be. Either in the office that Melissa used or in the kitchen, with its sprawling weathered pine table and four-door Aga.

She headed straight to the kitchen and hit the jackpot. Because there he was.

Georgina paused in the doorway and her breathing slowed and her heartbeat accelerated. He was staring out of the kitchen window at the inky black rain-lashed gardens, only visible when lightning flashed, illuminating the bending trees and shrubs.

He was still half naked but had slung on his jeans, which rode low on his lean hips. From behind, he was all muscle and sinew and bronzed streamlined beauty.

She padded towards him and knew exactly when

he became aware of her presence, because he stilled and then he turned around, very slowly, and looked at her in silence.

He broke the silence to ask her in a roughened undertone, 'What are you doing here?'

He hadn't been working. Only one light was switched on, over the kitchen table, so that he was enveloped in semi-darkness. Confused, Georgina wondered whether he'd just been staring out of the window and thinking. Thinking about what? *Her?*

She held on to that thought because it gave her the courage to stand there in front of him, back in her jeans just as he was, but with the too-tight top an open invitation—whether he realised that or not.

He realised.

He stepped towards her into the light and his eyes dropped to her breasts, lingered there, lingered on the shape of them, their heavy weight and the prominence of her nipples pushing against the thin stretchy fabric.

When eventually his eyes collided with hers, they registered what she was struggling to vocalise.

'Well?'

He took another step towards her, poetry in motion, his dark, brooding beauty sending shivers through her.

'Did you want something to drink? Water?'

'I couldn't get to sleep,' Georgina whispered, moving towards him.

'No?'

Matias paused, just out of reaching distance. It was going to be up to her to close the gap. He'd laid his cards on the table, told her that he wanted her, and she had turned him away. Now he was in charge, and this was his way of telling her that if she wanted him she was going to have to make the first move.

But what if he'd lost interest in the interim?

Georgina shut down that train of thought immediately. She was here and she was going to take what she'd wanted to have for...*for ever*...

'No. I started to think...'

'Thinking can sometimes be a dangerous luxury.'

'Certainly dangerous...' She stepped towards him, and she was breathing thickly as she placed one flattened palm against his chest. 'Because I was thinking about *you*—thinking about the fact that I want you. Matias, I don't want to play it safe. You're dangerous... I know that...but I want to know... I *need* to know...'

Her voice trailed off and uncertainly she kept her hand where it was, not knowing what the outcome of this was going to be, but knowing that she had to risk possible rejection to find out.

'You need to know what it feels like to take a walk on the wild side...?'

'Something like that,' Georgina muttered inaudibly.

She made to remove her hand, already smelling rejection, but then he took her hand in his and tugged her towards him, a little closer, close enough for her to feel the warmth of his breath on her face.

'You're right about me, Georgie. I'm dangerous. And what you're doing right now… It's called playing with fire.'

'I know,' she whispered. 'But maybe I've lived too long telling myself that playing it safe is the only way for me. I've been so careful not to take chances as far as guys are involved but you're right. Being careful might make sense, but sometimes making sense can be a joyless exercise. You don't tick any of my boxes…'

'Who's interested in a checklist?'

'I always have been,' she breathed. 'Especially after Robbie. I felt like he slipped through the net. You're right. My parents approved and I suppose I felt at the time that making them proud was important. After all…' She laughed self-consciously. 'I spent my life not living up to their expectations. At least that was what I thought, deep down. Never bright enough. Bit of a disappointment, really. So Robbie came along, and they approved, and that counted for a lot… And then…'

And then there was you…there was always you… And who's to say that Robbie wasn't my way of trying to escape from the stranglehold you'd always seemed to have over me…?

It occurred to her in a revelatory flash that maybe, beyond the whole lust thing, doing this…taking this step…*making love to this man*…would snuff out the hold he'd always seemed to exercise over her. The unknown was so tantalising, wasn't it? Matias had always been her fantasy guy, but as soon as he became a known quantity she would be free of him, in a manner of speaking. He would no longer be a dream inside her head, an untested benchmark against which other men had always been found wanting.

'And then...?' he was asking her now, in that dark voice, rich as the richest chocolate, that could make the hairs on the back of her neck stand on end.

'And then, when it all fell apart, I sat back and took stock and told myself that I would never make the same mistake again. Next time round I would go out with someone I felt was suited to *me*. Someone who had all the qualities I looked for. Someone on *my* wavelength.'

'But now you like the thought of playing with fire...?'

'Have *you* ever played with fire?'

'Not when it comes to sex,' Matias murmured huskily. 'I've had one or two nail-biting moments with deals that hung in the balance, but I like knowing where I am when it comes to relationships. We need to go upstairs, Georgie. We need a bed...'

Their eyes tangled, and in the soft light, with the steady drumbeat of the rain against the windows, something inside Georgina twisted. This was the point, she knew, when decisions would be made and there would be no going back.

So she would be taking a risk? But where had being careful got her? This fake relationship was the closest thing she'd got to adventure in years. This man standing in front of her was the closest thing she'd got to exciting in even longer. He wasn't right for her and he didn't try and pretend otherwise. He fancied her because… She didn't quite know why, but he seemed to… And, God, did she fancy *him*. He took her breath away. Always had.

She could fight the attraction but this was her moment, her window. If she walked away now then he wouldn't look back, but she would always wonder. *He* wouldn't, but *she* would. He wanted a bed and so did she.

But first…

She ran her hands along his thighs. She couldn't miss the thick bulge of his erection. A surge of feminine power rushed through her in a wave and she stifled a groan. She laid her hand on it and heard him hiss at the touch, although he kept himself perfectly still.

Eventually he clasped some of her bright, tangled hair in his hand and gently drew her face up so that they were staring at one another.

'Think hard,' he murmured, 'because you'll be stepping out of your comfort zone. My mother thinks we're having a relationship, but we both know the truth…'

'I get it, Matias. This isn't for real. I'm not going to start getting confused and delusional. How many times do you think you have to hint at that before you realise that you're preaching to the converted?' Her voice was strangled, because thinking straight was proving impossible when the evidence of his attraction to her was pulsing against her hand.

'Let's go upstairs,' Matias urged, his breathing ragged. 'The way you're touching me… I need to get these jeans off. I need to feel you…taste you…take you… I want to be inside you, Georgie, hot and hard.'

'Matias…'

'That's nice…'

He kissed her long and hard and deep, until she could scarcely breathe. She just couldn't get enough of that dragging, hungry kiss.

'I like it when you say my name like that… I like the sound of you wanting me as much as I want you… I'd take you right here on this kitchen table, but we'll have to save the adventure for when we have a bit more privacy.'

He drew back, and the hungry darkness in his eyes made her giddy with excitement.

'For now… Let's go upstairs…'

CHAPTER SEVEN

THEY MADE IT up the stairs softly and quickly, any noise drowned out by the pounding of the rain outside. The click of the bedroom door shutting behind them made her shudder with anticipation.

'I need to see you.' Matias moved to switch on one of the lamps, bathing the room in a mellow glow. 'I want to see every inch of your glorious body when I make love to you.'

This felt like tasting forbidden fruit, and now that she had succumbed to temptation her excitement levels were rising fast. Georgina looked at him as he walked towards her. He touched her and she curved into him, and for a few seconds they held one another without saying anything.

Then, 'I'm not the skinny catwalk model type,' she murmured against him.

'You're not.' He propelled her towards the bed without breaking contact.

'You *like* skinny catwalk model types.'

'Is this based on your close observation of me over the years?'

Georgina reddened, and he laughed softly and kissed the side of her mouth.

'You're wondering,' he murmured, 'whether to tell me that I'm an egotistical swine...'

'If the hat fits...' But she smiled nervously, and as the back of her knees came into contact with the mattress she collapsed onto the bed, eyes darkening as he remained standing, began unzipping the jeans.

Her arms were spread wide, her hair a vibrant mane across the pillow. The jeans came off, and then the boxers. and she drew in a sharp breath when he circled his penis with his hand and gently played with himself while he watched her with smouldering intensity.

Drugged with desire, Georgina discovered a side to herself she'd never known existed. A side without inhibition...a side that wanted to touch, to lick, to taste, to feel her own wetness the way he was feeling his own arousal.

Gone was the primness that had held her in check all her life and in its place was a wanton, bold, daring woman who wanted to explore every inch of the man now settling onto the bed next to her.

'Too many clothes,' Matias said thickly, and he undressed her at speed, rearing up as he tugged down her jeans, taking her underwear with them, and then the too-tiny top.

For a long moment he stared at her. He adored her with his eyes and she couldn't breathe for wanting him.

'Good God,' he said in a driven undertone. 'So damned beautiful…so bloody sexy…where have you been all my life?'

It was just a figurative way of speaking, but, oh, how she wanted to shout, *Here… I've always been here…*

It was so erotic, such a turn-on, and the heat pooled wet between her legs. He straddled her and gently swept her hair back, so that he could trail delicate kisses along her neck and enjoy the hitch in her breathing and her soft purrs of pleasure.

His movements were slow, leisurely, intensely arousing. His touch was delicate, but she knew that there was sheathed power behind the light touch. He was taking his time.

He covered her mouth with his and began kissing her, tasting her, probing the inside of her mouth with his tongue while he idly stroked her belly. Her generous breasts begged to be touched, and if by not touching them he intended to ratchet up her frantic desire to have him then he was spot-on.

'So bloody beautiful,' he murmured raggedly.

She laughed with her eyes as they broke apart for a few seconds. 'You don't mean that.'

'I never say anything I don't mean.'

'No, you don't, do you?' Georgina's breathing was shallow and she wriggled sinuously against him, like a cat responding to the bliss of being stroked. 'You don't care how your words affect other people, do you?'

'Life's a tough business.' Matias looked down at her for a few seconds, his dark eyes impenetrable. 'I spent my early life moving away from my parents' hocus-pocus lifestyle choices, and I discovered along the way that focusing on the tangible is all that matters. Caring too much about the abstract is a recipe for disaster.'

'You mean love…?'

'It gets in the way of what's really important in life.'

'Which is what?'

'Too much talk.' Matias neatly sidestepped the question, but then shot her a crooked smile because her questioning green eyes refused to be deflected. 'You don't give up, do you? I don't do *love*, Georgie. My head rules my life. Always been that way and always will be that way. I've seen first-hand what happens when you start thinking with your emotions. You end up with a chaotic, rudderless life. Don't look at me as though I've put out a hit on Father Christmas!' He laughed softly. 'Now, stop talking and let me pleasure you… You don't have to feel nervous with me,' he soothed.

'I'm not,' Georgina lied.

'Now who's telling fibs? You're tensing up. I can feel it.'

'I'm not what you're used to. Physically.'

'So you've already reminded me—and, no, you're not,' Matias responded with honesty. 'But I say that as the greatest of compliments. I like your body…so sexy…a man could lose himself in your curves… I can't begin to tell you just what I want to do to you…'

'I'm not experienced…'

'I'm not looking for experience.'

He couldn't hold off any longer and he covered her breast with his hand, played with her stiffened nipple, rubbing it and feeling it pucker between his fingers. He was so close to having an orgasm just from touching her like this that he was seriously shocked.

'Matias…'

'Shh…'

'I've never done this before,' Georgina said in a rush, and Matias went completely still.

She held her breath and wished that she could yank that admission right back into her mouth and bury it. She wanted him more than she'd ever thought it was possible to want anyone, but was he going to want to make love to a virgin?

She'd never given a huge amount of thought to the fact that she'd never slept with a man. She'd never been the sort of girl to be seduced by the thought of sleeping around. Then, when she'd met Robbie, she hadn't wanted to rush into bed with him. It had been important to her to take her time. She'd been pleased that he hadn't tried to force her hand. She could see now that he just hadn't been as attracted to her as she'd hoped, and vice versa. They'd both jumped into something for the wrong reasons. But now…

'When you say…?'

'I haven't done this before. Robbie and I...' She faltered in embarrassment and looked away, but Matias gently turned her so that she was looking at him.

He rolled onto his side and manoeuvred her onto hers so that they were facing one another. 'But you were a serious item...'

'I know,' Georgina said in a small voice.

She wished she'd never opened her mouth now. Because would he have *guessed* that she was a virgin? She could have pretended...bitten back any cries of pain if it hurt when he entered her. Judging from what she could see, he was impressive when it came to size. She felt like an idiot.

'No sex... That should have been the writing on the wall for you...'

'It's not *always* about sex,' Georgina protested helplessly.

'Oh, but it really is. And after Robbie...? Was there no one who could tempt you between the sheets?'

Georgina squirmed. 'I've been busy,' she muttered, her face as hot as a furnace and as red as a beetroot. She took a deep breath and gave him an out clause. 'I'll understand if you don't want to proceed any further.'

'What are you talking about?'

'You're used to stunningly beautiful women who would have lost their virginity in their teens...'

'I'd be your first...' Matias said, with a certain amount of wonder. He felt a surge of desire, a naked, raw craving rush through him in a tidal wave. 'I'm going to be honest with you…'

'Of course,' Georgina said miserably.

'I haven't been so turned on in my entire life.'

He was swept by the uncomfortable thought that a woman with no experience, a woman with romantic notions, might likewise be a woman with a heart waiting to be broken. But then he remembered how vehement she had been in her conviction that he wasn't her type, and how readily she had accepted the rules of this game, and the errant moment of unease was gone.

This was a flash in the pan. A really thrilling, rush-of-adrenaline flash in the pan. For *both* of them. It would burn out, they would go their separate ways and that would be that. She would meet her Mr Right in due course. If she lost her virginity to him then she would be in good hands—because he would be gentle with her. Many wouldn't. Furthermore, they *knew* one another. They had history.

'Really?' Georgina asked.

'Really—and enough talking.'

He would do his utmost to slow down, but temptation was like a banquet put in front of a starving beggar.

Georgina luxuriated in the sight of his lean, glorious beauty. In the shadows, his body was all angles and strength, bronzed and powerful. When he straddled her, the feel of his thick, pulsing erection filled her with wonder…with dark excitement…and with sharp apprehension all at the same time.

She was shocked by the graphic direction of her thoughts. Her lack of curiosity before when it came to sex astounded her. Curiosity was tearing her apart now. She felt as though she was waking up and coming alive for the first time in her life.

'Enjoying the sight?' Matias teased.

'You're very big…' she breathed, with honesty, and he burst out laughing and settled alongside her, turning her so that they were facing one another.

He sobered up. 'Don't be afraid. I'll be gentle, and the female body is fashioned to take a man of my size. Relax and you'll enjoy the ride. I promise you.'

He kissed her, kissed every inch of her face— soft kisses that melted her from the inside out. If she was nervous about making love, his touch was dismantling those nerves and sending her inhibitions to the four winds.

She wriggled and fell back as he pinned her hands above her head and then began kissing her again— her shoulders, her neck, her breasts, nibbling and licking, and then, when she could take no more of the rising excitement, he took one throbbing nipple into his mouth. He moistened it with his tongue, teasing the stiffened bud until she wanted to scream. He nipped it gently, suckled, drawing it into his mouth then moving on to pay attention to the other.

He stilled her when all she wanted to do was thrash around, and when she was still he cupped her between her legs, waiting and then slowly insinuating his finger into her, feeling her wetness, gliding over it and finding the tight bud of her clitoris.

Georgina couldn't stand it. Nothing had ever felt so good. She felt a burst of intense pleasure begin rippling through her as his finger glided between her thighs, smoothing the velvety crease there. She parted her legs and moved against his finger. Her body arched up and he continued to lick and tease her protuberant nipples.

There was no question that he knew what to do with a woman's body, how to electrify it on all fronts, how to make it twist and wriggle with pleasure.

With a groan of self-restraint Georgina pulled back from that devastating finger and applied herself to giving *him* some of the pleasure he had been giving her. Inexperience made her hesitate, but the driving need to feel him was greater than any insecurities on that front.

She cupped him in her hands and, kneeling, took his bigness into her mouth. She felt a thrill of delight at his immediate response. She could tell that he couldn't resist what she was doing to him and that gave her a heady sense of pure feminine power.

Every muscle in his body tensed as she continued to lick and suck him, while her own enflamed body had time to cool down a little. Just a little.

His deep moans thrilled her. The way he clasped her hair, guiding her, thrilled her. Everything about this guy thrilled her in ways she couldn't define.

She licked his shaft and he uttered a stifled groan.

'My God, Georgie…' His voice was unsteady, his breathing uneven. 'I can't think straight when you're doing that.'

Georgina broke off to say, 'Good,' before picking up where she'd left off.

'This isn't going according to plan…' He tugged himself free of her exploring mouth and took a few seconds to gather himself before staring down at her with dark amusement. 'Speed wasn't on the agenda.'

Sprawled back on the pillow, arms spread, Georgina stared at him from under her lashes with drowsy delight, her body moving to its own beat because she just couldn't seem to keep still.

'I'm so desperate for you,' she moaned.

'In case you've missed it,' Matias said roughly, 'the feeling's mutual.'

He began groping for his wallet, cursing softly under his breath until he'd extracted protection.

Where was his fabled cool? Nowhere in evidence, Georgina realised with a rush of satisfaction. His hands were trembling as he donned the condom and his movements were urgent as he settled over her.

He entered her gently, and she knew that he was exercising extreme restraint. Bit by bit he inched his bigness into her wetness, slowing when she tensed, then pushing more firmly as she accommodated his girth.

'So fantastically tight and wet,' he groaned. 'You're driving me crazy, woman.'

Her groans were fast little puffs as he sank deeper into her, and then he was moving fast and hard.

Georgina winced. Then the fierce discomfort of that initial thrust was overwhelmed by the exquisite sensations racing through her as he picked up pace. His girth and size, which she had eyed with some apprehension, was the very thing that felt so good now that he was deep inside her.

Somehow, without their bodies parting an inch, he manoeuvred her so that she was on top of him, her full breasts dangling down to his waiting mouth. Her body knew what to do and it was the most amazing thing. She knew how to move, how to gyrate on him until the need to come was so overpowering that she could no longer resist.

The orgasm that swept her away was shattering. She heard herself cry out as she arched back—a soft, urgent cry—and she knew that he was coming as well, because she could feel the rigid tension in his powerful body, the stiffening just before release, and then she collapsed against him, utterly and completely replete.

Matias broke the silence. 'That was…amazing.'

Warm and drowsy after the racing fury of her orgasm, Georgina curled against him, enjoying his warmth and the lean, muscular angles of his body. This was a dream come true. It felt that way. Yes, it was dangerous, but it felt so good, so *right*. She wanted to shout from the rooftops that it had been better than amazing for her, that she was now *complete*.

'Lovely,' she said instead, and she felt him grin against her neck.

'Try not to go overboard with enthusiasm,' he said drily, but his voice was amused and teasing, his dark eyes slumberous and warm as he looked at her.

'I won't,' Georgina replied, equally lightly. 'Your ego is big enough, Matias Silva, without me swelling it even further.'

'I'll take that as your quirky way of telling me that the earth moved for you.' He nibbled her ear, then her neck, then smoothed his hand along her warm, soft body, taking his time to feel every glorious inch of her.

Outside, the fierce tempo of the rain had faded into a soft patter. And into this comforting background noise several questions began to raise their tiresome heads. Top of the list was...*what happens now?*

'I'm going to go have a shower...' It was the only thing Georgina could think of to say as her head began to whirl. 'Er...we should get some sleep... and then tomorrow... Well, you never know with the weather round here. You wouldn't believe how long the rain can last. Flooding. Roads under water. But it sounds like it's beginning to fade...'

'Thanks for the weather update.'

Matias grinned, holding her in place next to him, and Georgina was horrified to discover how much she liked that possessive arm pinning her to the spot.

'Why are you going to have a shower?'

'Because...'

'Don't even *think* about getting dressed.' He stroked her thigh and slipped his hand between her legs, so that he could play absently with the soft, fuzzy hair there. 'We're not done yet... How's the foot doing, by the way? I hope things weren't too energetic for you...'

'Foot?'

'Ah, good. You've forgotten. I'm taking that to mean you haven't given it a passing thought. I don't want to tire you, or hurt you if you're sore, but I want you again, Georgie. I don't know what you've done to me...you're a witch.'

'Matias...'

Suddenly she was reading all sorts of things into his carelessly delivered words. *The sex was amazing... where had she been all his life?...she'd cast a spell on him like a witch...*

Like a horse breaking free of its restraints her imagination was playing fast and loose with reality, and even as she tried to rein it in she could feel its perilous temptation towards a fairy tale ending that was never in a million years going to happen.

Heart beating like a sledgehammer, she pulled back from the seductive allure of his caresses to meet his eyes in the darkened room. 'This was never supposed to happen, Matias. We got carried away and one thing led to another. I'm not completely naïve. I know these things happen.'

'You're right when you say that this wasn't on the

cards. But it's on the cards now.' He slid his finger into her wet crease and felt her little spasm of delight. 'And don't try and tell me that this is a one-off, that we've got to put the whole thing behind us because "one thing led to another". Your body is telling me that you're as hot for me right now as I am for you.'

'That's not the point…'

'Then what is?'

'Our sleeping together could lead to all sorts of complications.'

'Personally,' Matias returned wryly, 'I think that you ringing on my doorbell and telling me that we're an item was a lot more fraught with complications. I wanted you. I want you now. And I'm not going to have a shower and then pretend that this never happened.'

'So what do you suggest?'

Georgina gasped as he found the stiffened bud of her clitoris and gently began to rub the pad of his finger over it.

'I can't think properly when you're doing that…'

'Good. Because this isn't about thinking. This is about the two of us giving in to something that's bigger than both of us.'

'It doesn't make sense…'

She began to move against his finger, her body disobeying her brain as she'd known it would. She'd barely come down from the splintering high of orgasm and she could already feel little spasms of mounting pleasure as he rubbed her. Her nipples ached and she pictured his dark head nuzzling and suckling at her breasts. That turned her on even more.

'Let's agree not to question this, Georgie. So what if it doesn't make sense? We got on this rollercoaster and I think we should just go along for the ride. When the ride comes to an end we'll deal with it…'

'You should at least think about it,' Rose was saying as she fussed around them.

They had come for breakfast—a routine that had been established ever since they had arrived, a week ago. Their nights were spent together at Georgina's house. Their days were largely spent with Rose. Time was galloping past and Georgina had decided that uncomfortable thoughts were best left unexplored.

She'd made big decisions. She'd chosen to carry on sleeping with Matias instead of doing what her head had told her to do, which was to write off that single night at Melissa's as an anomaly. She'd made loads of excellent arguments to support her decision, but now that the decision had been made what was the point of tormenting herself with pointless speculation about whether she'd done the right thing or not?

Besides, with each passing day Rose seemed to have a renewed lease of life, and Georgina knew that the openly touchy-feely stuff between herself and Matias partially accounted for that.

They were no longer involved in a charade—at

least not as far as the physical side of things went—and maybe she had picked up on some intangible vibes and was responding to them. Who knew?

Right now Rose was waiting for a response to a question that had the potential to open up a can of worms.

Sprawled in a chair, long legs stretched out in front of him and crossed loosely at the ankles, Matias was watching Georgie from under luxuriant dark lashes and maintaining an unhelpful silence.

'It wouldn't work,' Georgina said awkwardly as she began to clear the table. 'I mean, Rose, so much of my work is tied up here... I couldn't just ditch all of that and move to...er...London. It's a dog-eat-dog world there and I'm just a minnow. I'd be eaten alive.'

She paused after that bagful of mixed metaphors and tried to garner support from Matias with a meaningful look. He returned her stare without taking the bait.

Rose's face fell. 'But then I just don't see how things are going to work between the two of you.' She looked at Matias with a hint of apology. 'I know you hate talking about things like this, Matias, and I hope you won't be offended...'

Matias waved a casual hand and shifted ever so slightly. 'Feel free, Mother. I don't want you to think that you have to edit your words because of me.'

'Well, I do understand that all those clandestine meetings in London must have been terribly exciting...'

She paused fractionally to look at Georgina, who duly responded, 'Terribly...'

'But after the first excitement relationships have to grow and mature. You're both here now, and I can see with my own eyes just how much enjoyment the pair of you find in one another. You're in one another's company all the time and I think that's giving you so many opportunities to really deepen the connection between you. In fact, I've seen that with my own two eyes! I've seen the way you look at each other!'

Out of the corner of her eye Georgina was aware of Matias's discomfort at this perfectly reasonable observation from his mother and a dart of malicious satisfaction streaked through her.

He was absolutely in favour of them continuing their relationship while he was enjoying the sex, and because of that he had jettisoned all plans to engineer their situation towards an eventual break-up. Was it any wonder that his mother was now beginning to look beyond the present to the future?

'It's going to end up being impractical if you have to conduct a long-distance relationship. Those things seldom work. It's far too easy to be tempted by someone else if the person you love is a thousand miles away.'

'Cornwall isn't a thousand miles away from London,' Georgina pointed out. 'And,' she added for good measure, 'if a guy is tempted just because there's a bit of distance between himself and the woman he's supposed to be madly in love with, then he wasn't madly in love in the first place.'

Rose knew her son, and she knew very well that Matias had always been short on commitment and big on variety when it came to women. Georgina could understand perfectly well why she was worried about the distance between them, but there was no way she was going to pretend that her migrating to London was an option. *No way.*

And wasn't this a good excuse to start sowing the seeds of what might go wrong between the love birds?

It had been so easy over the past few days to be lulled into thinking that there was an element of *reality* about all this—but she and Matias had two very different takes on reality.

For her, reality was a relationship founded in commitment—a relationship that was going somewhere, developing into something that had a future. Something beyond sex.

For Matias, reality was taking what he wanted. It was sex and fun until the sex got boring and the fun began to peter out.

'Some might say that a long-distance relationship really siphons off the flash-in-the-pan romance from the slow burn of something long-lasting. Wouldn't you agree, Matias?'

Matias shrugged and raised his eyebrows.

'Your mother has a point, don't you think? Clandestine is all very well and good, but when the thrill of that is over and done with, what next?'

Silence greeted this provocative remark, and Georgina bit down hard on a hiss of impatience.

The telephone trilled from the hallway, breaking the silence, which had continued to stretch.

Rose scuttled out of the kitchen.

'You're breathing fire,' Matias drawled. 'Care to tell me why?'

'Why do you *think*, Matias?'

'My mother does have a point,' he agreed mildly. 'If you want your career to develop beyond doing a few shoots for the chef down the road, then you're eventually going to have to head for the big, bad city lights.'

'You *know* that's not what she was talking about!'

She clicked her tongue with annoyance. How could he just lounge there, sprawled in that chair with that half-smile on his face, looking so drop-dead gorgeous when he should be taking her seriously? She knew that if he'd already got sick of her, if the sex had run its course, then he would be leaping onto the exit strategy she had tried to set in motion.

'True,' Matias was honest enough to admit.

'We need to prepare the way for your mother to realise that this isn't going to end up where she thinks it is. Matias, read between the lines. Rose is building up to this being more than just a relationship. Why didn't you follow my lead?'

'I've always hated the concept of being a follower.'

'I'm being serious!' Georgina cried with frustration.

Matias pressed his fingers against his eyes, and

when he looked at her it was with bone-wrenching gravity. 'I know you are,' he said in a low voice. 'And, trust me, I fully appreciate the wisdom of what you were trying to do. But…'

He raked his fingers through his hair and for the first time since she had known him Georgina could see that he was grappling to express what he wanted to say. In a man as fluent, as lazily sophisticated and utterly controlled and self-assured as Matias Silva, it was a sight that left her temporarily lost for words.

'But…?' she encouraged, when nothing further seemed to be forthcoming.

He straightened in the chair and raked his fingers through his hair. 'But this whole charade has gone down an unexpected route.'

'I don't understand…'

'My mother was depressed. I found myself somehow cajoled into a role I hadn't auditioned for…'

'I *get* that, Matias.' The last thing Georgina felt she needed was a reminder of just how much of an unwilling participant he had been in this whole charade. 'Which is why—'

'Hear me out, Georgie. I thought that once my mother was back in the land of the living—mentally— we could bring this whole game to a timely end. I hadn't banked on my relationship with my mother veering off in unforeseen directions.' He shifted uncomfortably and looked at her broodingly. 'We've spent a lifetime plodding along,' Matias said heavily. 'Always polite, always distant.'

His voice was so low that she had to move close to him to hear what he was saying. Having sat down, she felt her knees almost touching his, and she was leaning into him, her bright hair pulled over one shoulder.

He absently tugged at the curling ends of her hair, twirling strands around his finger while he continued to hold her gaze. It was a gesture of unbearable intimacy and it went straight to the very core of her, even though she knew she was reading way too much into it.

'I spent half a lifetime pulling away from my parents,' he said ruefully. 'In the end we simply inhabited different worlds. My father could never understand it, and my deepest regret is that it became a rift that was never resolved. With my mother... Well, I suppose I tried to heal that rift by making sure no expense was spared. Whatever she wanted, she got.'

He shrugged.

'Now, though, that rift is healing, and it's an unexpected by-product of this little charade of ours. I've never been closer to my mother. That's why I chose not to take you up on the very considerate rescue package you were putting into motion.' He leaned back and shot her a crooked half-smile. 'I can see that you're moved by my uncustomary outpouring of confidences...'

'I think it's brilliant that you and your mother are

finding a way forward…' Georgina wanted to tack a diplomatic *but* on the end of that remark, but then she looked at him, at his guarded expression, and her heart twisted.

She gazed back helplessly at him and he pulled her towards him and kissed her.

Conversation closed.

CHAPTER EIGHT

GEORGINA WASN'T SURE what had been resolved by their hurried conversation.

Would the opportunity arise for her to try and get some sort of timeline for their relationship that should never have been? Did Matias even *do* time-lines? And if she pushed him…what then?

Thoughts whirled in her head, sparking off one another, one confused thought leading to another.

She didn't want this to end. She wanted a timeline so that she could brace herself for the inevitable, but she didn't want the inevitable to come.

That realisation of weakness snaked through her, terrifying, implacable and revelatory.

This wasn't about lust. Maybe it had started there—although when Georgina thought about it she knew, in her heart, that there had been far more than lust when she had stepped out into the unknown and lost her virginity to Matias.

Yes, he was sexy—and, yes, he had touched her and her whole body had come alive. But she'd never been the sort of girl who was seduced by good looks and a bit of charm. Fact was, Matias had won her heart. And he'd won it, without even trying, a long time ago. Making love to him had been the final stage in a journey that had begun when she had been an impressionable teenager.

For him, she had become just like any one of his other women. Yes, they had history—so maybe not *quite* the same—and, yes, the circumstances behind their relationship were different, but in the end she was sleeping with him on his terms, ceding to something that was going to end because he wasn't into relationships or commitment.

She remembered the towering blonde in the small dress who had been in the process of being dispatched. She remembered rolling her eyes when Matias had said something about her being better off without him.

Here she was. At some point in time he would end up dispatching her in exactly the same way— probably when he thought that the charade they'd begun was no longer required. He'd never guess that she'd fallen in love with him and Georgina shuddered at the thought of him ever finding out.

'Where is she?' Georgina frowned and glanced to the door which Rose had pulled shut behind her when she had gone to pick up the telephone.

Matias looked down at her and then outlined her mouth with his finger, gently tugging at her bottom lip and making her shiver with sudden electric excitement when he inserted his finger into her mouth so that she could suck on it, mimicking what she did to his erection when they were together, naked.

Her mind went blank for a few seconds.

Forgetting to think whenever he touched her was becoming a lifestyle choice.

'We should go and find her.' Georgina managed to draw back and shoot him a stern look from under her lashes.

'If you insist,' Matias drawled, 'although, given this little window, I could think of one or two things I'd rather be doing…'

'Matias!'

'Will you ever stop being shocked at perfectly innocent statements?' He grinned but didn't remove his hand from where it was caressing the side of her neck. 'Or blushing? No, you'll never stop blushing. You've been doing that since you were a kid.'

'I can't help it,' Georgina mumbled. 'It must be a novelty for you, Matias.'

She thought of the Amazonian blonde, so beautiful, so experienced, so *with-it*. She began walking towards the door, her fingers lightly linked with his, as if her body had been programmed to keep touching his whenever and wherever possible.

'You're not kidding.' He tugged her to a stop and stared down at her thoughtfully. 'I haven't had too many dealings with women who blush at the mention of sex.'

'I don't do that!'

'You're doing it now.'

'Do you like it?'

'A change is always as good as a rest...'

Georgina subdued a little dart of pain. *Who wants to be a novelty in someone else's life?* she wondered. *Especially when you're in love with that someone and want nothing more than to be a permanent fixture?*

She plastered a rueful smile on her face and turned away.

'I've never made love to a virgin before, either,' he murmured, pulling her briefly against him and smiling.

'Notch on the bedpost, Matias?'

He frowned. 'Don't say that.'

'Why not? It's true, isn't it?'

'Do you want to start an argument with me?'

'Of course I don't.'

Georgina looked down, but he wouldn't allow that, tipping her chin so that she was forced to meet his gaze.

She looked back at him with a veiled expression, then said, her voice cooler, 'But we're both into being honest about what's going on here.' She shrugged. 'This is all for your mum, and I'm really happy that it's ended up being about more than just bringing her out of her mental slump. I'm really happy that along the way the two of you have finally managed to forge a meaningful connection.'

'What does that have to do with you thinking that

you're a notch on my bedpost because you were a virgin when we first made love?'

Georgina wished that he would stop going on about her virginity. It wasn't his intention, but did he have any idea how much the mention of her virginity led her to comparisons with all those women he had bedded who *hadn't* been virgins? She hated thinking of him in bed with other women. She'd never had a jealous bone in her body before, but right now her entire skeletal frame was glued together by the green-eyed monster.

'It was just an expression,' she said lightly.

'I *don't* see women as notches on my bedpost,' Matias persisted.

She could almost smile at his outraged expression. He'd said to her in passing that when it came to women he always laid his cards on the table, was always open and up-front with them. No commitment, no cosy meals in, no meeting the parents. If they chose to ignore those ground rules, then that wasn't his fault. He had a black and white approach to relationships that beggared belief.

'Let's drop this conversation. It's not going anywhere.'

She opened the door to a silent house, but instead of following Matias remained standing behind her, then he leaned down and whispered into her ear.

'You're not a notch on my bedpost—and don't put yourself down by saying something like that.'

'Who says I mind being a notch on your bedpost?' Georgina pointed out calmly.

That deepened his disapproving frown which, in turn, gave her a weird kind of kick. She raised her eyebrows and succumbed to something wicked inside her.

'I mean…' She dragged the syllables out as she looked at him without blinking. 'If I'm going to be a notch on anybody's bedpost, then who's to say that I don't want it to be yours?'

'This conversation is really beginning to get on my nerves, Georgie.'

'Why?'

'Don't give me that *butter-wouldn't-melt-in-my-mouth* expression,' he growled in return.

'I wasn't. I'm just saying…' she paused and tilted her head to one side '…that if I had to lose my virginity then there's no one in the world I'd rather have lost it to.' She said that with heartfelt sincerity. But little did he know just how sincere those words were, and before he started circling the truth and zooming in on it, like a hawk spying a sparrow, she added lightly, 'You're a fantastic lover. You've given me confidence. And when I look ahead…'

'Look ahead?'

'Well, you know…to when this is all over and I move on…'

'I don't speculate about events that have yet to come—so, no, I *don't* know.'

'Well, one day I'll meet the man I'll want to settle

down with—a man who's going to love me the way
I love him and want to settle down with me the way
I want to settle down with him—and when that hap-
pens I'm going to think back to—'

'I get the picture,' Matias snapped, flushing
darkly. 'No need to expand. And if this isn't the
sound of you wanting to start an argument, then I
don't know what is.'

'I have no idea why you're angry.'

'Whoever said anything about being angry?'

His dark eyes collided with hers and she swal-
lowed painfully.

'I just don't think that this is the time or the place
to start a soul-searching conversation about some
man who has yet to appear on your horizon.'

'You're right.'

Matias scowled. 'Yes.' His voice was tight and
clipped. 'I am.'

'Let's go and hunt down your mother—but before
we do I just want to say that I'm willing to go along
with this business of not sowing the seeds of discon-
tent because you feel you're finally building a relationship with your mother. But at some point we're
going to have to put a timeline on this…'

'And we will,' Matias inserted smoothly. 'Now,
let's drop the subject and find my mother—before
she comes looking for us and discovers the love birds
in the middle of a row. And don't even *think* of saying that that would be just what the doctor ordered.'

She was whisked out of the sitting room, and before she'd had time to wonder why he was in such a foul mood, when all she'd done was reassure him that she wasn't going to become clingy and needy, even though she blushed and had been a virgin when they'd gone to bed together, they were in the kitchen.

Georgina had thought that they would find Rose doing what she seemed to enjoy doing—namely, preparing something for them to eat, with the television or radio on in the background.

They didn't. Rose was sitting at the kitchen table and staring off into the distance, ashen-faced and as still as a statue.

'I was just about to come and find you two,' she said quietly. 'But I wanted to have a few minutes to myself first.'

'What's going on?' Matias questioned urgently, while Georgina did what seemed to come naturally to people in tense situations...went to make a pot of tea.

Concern made her want to rush and sit next to Rose, hold her hand. Instinct told her that this time it was Matias who needed to do that—as he was doing now.

'That was the consultant on the phone,' Rose was saying, after clearing her throat and breathing deeply. 'Remember those tests I was waiting for results for? Well, it seems that I haven't been given the all-clear after all.'

'I'll get the guy on the phone now. Find out what's going on.'

'Matias, no.' She laid her hand on his and patted it. 'I'm more than capable of handling this situation.'

From where she was standing, Georgina thought that that looked very far from the truth. She met Matias's panicked gaze and her heart went out to him. He was so strong, and yet right now so vulnerable. And she could understand why. His newly burgeoning relationship with his mother was still as delicate as a green shoot finding the sun. He wasn't quite sure how to deal with her obvious distress. He had conditioned his responses for so long to be dispassionate. Would he be able to handle the depth of his emotions?

In a flash, Georgina realised that she seemed to be reading him so thoroughly, and she wondered whether this was a by product of her love.

Was it?

She rested a cup of tea in front of Rose and drew up a chair next to her. 'So, word for word, what did he say?'

'I need an operation,' Rose said flatly. 'And sooner rather than later.'

'You're scared,' Georgina said quietly, 'and I get that. You'd got your hopes up that you'd be given the all-clear. But there's nothing to be afraid of.' She could feel Matias's eyes on her. She took Rose's hand and held it between her own. 'If there was anything truly concerning they would be sending an ambulance over for you right now. *Are* they?'

Rose shook her head and relaxed a little.

'When are you due to go in?'

'He wanted to see me the day after tomorrow, but I managed to persuade him to see me this afternoon.'

'See?' Georgina said reassuringly. 'The day after tomorrow? I'll bet this operation will be as straightforward as pulling out a tooth.'

She heard herself saying all the right things, and in between Matias chipped in, but on this rare occasion, words didn't come easily for him.

'I just worry,' Rose concluded, sighing. 'However straightforward an operation it may or may not be, who knows what will happen? General anaesthetic carries risks—especially for someone like me whose health has been compromised. And there's another thing…'

'What's that?' Matias questioned in a roughened undertone.

'It's been so wonderful seeing the two of you together,' Rose began. Her eyes welled up and she looked away quickly. 'When Georgina told me that you were going out…well, I could hardly believe it.'

Georgina fidgeted, but remained smiling. 'Perhaps you should try and get a little rest?' she murmured. 'You've had a bit of a shock. I can bring your tea up to your bedroom…'

'I thought that it couldn't possibly be true. But I've watched you together and I've hardly been able to credit it. Matias, you're my son, and I love you very much, but I know what you're like with the ladies.'

Matias flushed.

Georgina watched with some amusement as he tried and failed to find a suitable response, resorting to raking his fingers through his hair and squirming ever so slightly in his chair. For the first time in his life he was being openly called out on his behaviour and he didn't know how to deal with it. That was obvious.

'You like variety. Your father and I… Well, we knew we were meant for one another from a very young age, and we never wavered in our conviction or in our love.'

'I… I… We're not all the same…'

Georgina thought that if ever a person had looked as though they were being slowly spit-roasted over an open fire, then that person was Matias. The look he shot her was positively despairing, and it sent his appeal for her shooting into the stratosphere. If her heart hadn't already been handed over to him, then it surely would have been handed over right at that very moment.

'If you intend to toss Georgie aside, Matias, then you must do it before I go under the knife. I don't think I would be able to make it through if I thought that you were going to break her heart. I've been praying and keeping my fingers crossed that this lovely relationship you have goes the distance, but I'd rather face the worst-case scenario *before* I have the operation than go under general thinking that I might wake up to find that you've decided to break up—'

'Rose!' Georgina interrupted brightly. 'I'm right here! You're talking as though I've left the room! I'm more than capable of taking care of myself should we…should we *both* decide that things aren't working out between us!' She did her best to look as cheerful as possible. 'You really shouldn't be worrying about any of this. You've got enough on your plate.'

'She's right,' Matias said seriously. 'This is the last thing you should be thinking about. Especially when…' His dark eyes roved over Georgina's face. 'Especially when,' he continued gravely, 'we've both been waiting for the right moment to announce our engagement.'

For a few seconds Georgina didn't register what Matias had said. She continued smiling her glassy, soothing smile, but then the smile fell away and hot red colour flooded her cheeks.

It seemed that Rose was congratulating them both…saying something about a ring… And it also seemed that Matias was answering. But their voices were coming from a long way away, and only penetrating her brain the way a very fuzzy light might penetrate dense fog. Her brain certainly felt very foggy.

She was barely aware of Matias escorting his mother upstairs, because somewhere along the line she appeared to have lost the power of speech and of coherent thought in general.

He reappeared after fifteen minutes and stood in

the doorway for a few seconds before strolling into the kitchen.

'Not exactly the reaction I was expecting,' he drawled, circling her before dropping into the chair facing hers and promptly leaning forward, arms on his thighs, legs spread apart. 'Where's all the girlish excitable chatter?'

'Matias...' Georgina blinked and then focused on him, still blinking like an owl. '*Engaged*? How could you tell your mother that we're *engaged*?'

Suddenly galvanised into action, she leapt to her feet, sprinted over to make sure that the kitchen door was firmly shut, and then positioned herself in front of Matias, hands on her hips, her green eyes glinting dangerously.

'What choice was there?' Matias countered without batting an eye. 'You heard her. She's terrified of the operation ahead of her—which, as it turns out, is to have a pacemaker fitted. A routine procedure. She's genuinely concerned that things between us are going to go belly-up—that I'm going to revert to my bad old ways, but only after I've well and truly broken your heart. I think she believes that if she's braced for the worst, then she can steel herself to face it.'

'So just like that you decided that you'd expand our relationship into something a thousand times more serious...?'

'I'll admit,' he said grudgingly, 'that I've done what I accused you of doing, when you showed up at my house and informed me that we were a loved-up, starry-eyed couple. I've involved you in something you hadn't anticipated. But this is just a temporary add-on that will take my mother past this hurdle...'

Georgina's mind was in freefall. *Engaged to Matias Silva?* Under normal circumstances it would have been a dream come true. Under these circumstances it was a complication he couldn't begin to understand. It shouldn't make a difference, but somehow it did. It was like being within touching distance of nectar, but knowing that you were never going to reach it.

'What's the problem?' Matias asked. 'You saw how she reacted.' He paused. 'My mother has never discussed my life choices. Naturally, I've always known she disapproves, but to hear that disapproval voiced for the first time...'

He shook his head and turned the full wattage of his attention onto Georgina.

For a few seconds she was lost. This was a Matias she'd never thought she'd see. He was actually confiding in her, telling her things about himself that she knew he would never have told anyone—would probably never have admitted to himself.

A little voice whispered inside her: *A pretend engagement...with a man you're in love with...a man who, for the first time, is opening up about himself...*

It was hard not to feel quietly privileged.

It was also dangerous. And she banked down the

seductive little voice that was beginning to question whether Matias perhaps felt more for her than he himself knew.

'It's a sign of how much closer you two have become in a short space of time,' she mused thoughtfully. 'She trusts you enough to say what's on her mind instead of holding it in.'

'So, back to the matter at hand.'

He slapped his thighs and stood up, all business now. That window of emotion had been shut. Georgina wished with all her heart that she could push it open again. Instead, she followed suit and moved to finish tidying the dishes.

'Back to the matter at hand?' she asked.

'Rings.'

'What about them?'

'We need to get one.'

'Why?'

'Come on, Georgie. An engaged woman always wears a rock on her finger.'

He moved to stand next to her and lifted her hand, inspected her finger.

She snatched her hand away. 'Surely that's taking the pretence too far? Has it occurred to you that when it comes to something as serious as an engagement I might actually want to wear a ring on my finger that *means* something? That's a declaration of intent from a guy who wants to go the whole hog and walk up the aisle with me?'

'No,' Matias said, dropping her hand and heading for the door, then spinning round on his heels to look at her before opening it. 'My mother's recommended some jewellers. I, personally, would rather get something in London, but perhaps a ring from somewhere local might carry more significance.'

'Did you hear a word I just said?'

'I heard every word. Are you telling me that you're not willing to go along with this?'

'No… I can see the upsides… I just thought you should know that—'

'Okay. Got it. Then let's go. We can wrap this up in a couple of hours. My mother's appointment with the consultant is later this afternoon. I'll want to accompany her. If she sees a ring on your finger her spirits will be good enough to deal with the details of the operation.'

He was back to being the Matias of old. Assured, in charge, emotions firmly under lock and key.

Despite spending most of his adult life anywhere other than Cornwall, he still knew the roads and streets like the back of his hand, and they were at the jeweller's within forty-five minutes of leaving the house.

'One of my mother's daughters designs bespoke rings here.' Matias killed the engine outside an exquisite chocolate box house on a side street, sandwiched between a bridal shop and a high-end shoe shop. He looked at her wryly. 'In between her concerns over this upcoming operation, she managed to impart *that* gem of information.'

Georgina was gazing at the shop front. 'Emily Thornton?' she said. 'Have you any idea how expensive her stuff is?'

'Have you any idea how little I care about that?' He reached across her to push open the passenger door, then remained staring at her for a few seconds. 'You look as jumpy as a cat on a hot tin roof. It's just part of this charade we've signed up to.'

'I realise that it doesn't mean anything…'

'So you shouldn't feel anxious. Now, let's go and see what the finest jeweller in the West Country has to offer, shall we?'

Squashing the temptation to attach any significance to the choosing of an engagement ring, and making sure to keep at the forefront of her mind Matias's flat reminder that this was all just a continuation of the game *she* had initiated, Georgina eyed the array of glittering jewels brought out for their inspection.

There were no prices on any of them—which was alarming. The quality was stunning, and her mouth was dry when she casually pointed to the most gaudy of the rings on display.

'Funny…' Matias murmured under his breath. 'That's the last ring I would have pictured you choosing.'

Georgina shrugged, but got the feeling that he knew exactly what was going through her mind— she intended to save choosing a ring she truly loved for a guy she really cared about. It was a twisted version of the truth, but she was determined to play this game as coolly as he was.

When it was slipped onto her finger she stared at it, while the young sales assistant oohed and ahhed and told her that she couldn't have chosen anything more beautiful.

'Why don't you try that one, my darling?' Matias removed the ring and returned it to the girl, his dark, amused eyes firmly fixed on Georgina's face. 'Personally, I think an oversized diamond squatting on a band of gold isn't right for your delicate finger.'

Their eyes tangled—and then he reached out and picked the very ring she would have chosen for herself.

'There, now…' He held her hand up and inspected it from all angles. 'Much better. We'll take it.'

He paid, and Georgina stared at the delicate strands of interwoven rose gold and the small perfect diamonds that followed the strands. When she twisted her hand ever so slightly the strands almost seemed to move, like a thread of liquid gold flowing over precious gems.

She shoved her hand down to her side, because when she looked at the ring the whole scenario felt way too real.

'Now,' Matias said, as they were leaving the shop, 'we'll collect my mother and take her to see the consultant.'

There was nothing romantic about this occasion. He had switched off the second they had left the jeweller's, and once in the car had promptly engaged himself in a lengthy conference call conducted partly in English, partly in Italian.

Georgina stared ahead, and started when he said, without looking at her, 'That gaudy bauble wouldn't have fooled someone as astute as my mother.'

'I still think we could have held off actually buying a ring. You could have said we wanted to choose something later, in London.'

'And deprive her of the pleasure of knowing that we'd found something locally? You know my mother when it comes to keeping it small and local. I have to admit she has a point when it comes to choosing a ring.' Without taking his eyes off the road he reached for her hand, held it up and glanced at the perfect band of gold. 'Like it?'

'It's fine.'

'You can keep it when this is all over.'

'Why would I want to do that?'

'Call it payment for services rendered.' He shrugged. 'But if you find that offensive, then by all means you can give it back to me. At any rate, we'll cross that bridge when we get to it.'

Georgina thought that he couldn't have succeeded better when it came to keeping things on a strictly business level.

She sat on her hand for the remainder of the journey to the house, staring straight ahead. Then it was all go as they took Rose to the hospital, where her consultant was waiting for her.

Her nerves were palpable, barely concealed under a flurry of questions about their choice of ring.

'It's going to be fine.'

Georgina continued to reassure the older woman and was pleased to notice, when they eventually reached the hospital, that she automatically reached for Matias's arm—a real indication of how much their relationship had progressed and confirmation that this make-believe engagement was the right thing to do.

The last thing Rose needed right now was the additional stress of worrying about Matias walking away. Not just walking away from *her*, Georgina now realised, but, in Rose's mind, walking away from the relationship which had slowly been building between herself and her son.

Did she perhaps think that a Matias returning to his former ways—a Matias whose only goal was making money, whose take on relationships was casual and dismissive—would also be a Matias who would no longer want to forge those filial bonds which had been missing for so many years?

Georgina sighed to herself, because it seemed as though by taking this step she and Matias might well have jumped from the frying pan straight into the fire. And, much as she wanted to adopt his approach to the situation, which was to take things one day at a time and only cross bridges when they got to them, she found herself chewing over all the worst-case scenarios that might arise.

While she waited for Matias and Rose to return from the lengthy consultation, she thought about the dangers inherent in this pretend situation that she so badly wanted to be real. She wondered how long they would continue the pretence…how long they would continue sleeping with one another. She felt helpless to end things. She wanted him so badly that she was willing to take whatever was on offer. And she hated herself for becoming so much like all those women who had preceded her.

And then there was the practical question of how they would conduct a long-distance relationship…

For the first time Georgina gave house room to thoughts of moving to London. Of course it was a nonsense, because she would never leave Cornwall to pursue the dream of being more to Matias than a casual affair. But if she were to be close at hand…

She was staring down at the ring on her finger when she heard footsteps and looked up to see Matias and his mother walking towards her.

'All booked for the day after tomorrow,' Matias said, looking from the engagement ring on her finger to the delicate bloom of colour in her cheeks.

'I thought I might as well get it over and done with.' Rose's voice was brighter than it had been. 'I've never believed in private healthcare, but I have to admit that it's a weight off my shoulders knowing that I don't have to wait weeks to have this operation. And, as Matias says, the sooner it's done, the sooner I can start enjoying wedding plans. That is, Georgie, if you won't find a middle-aged woman too intrusive? Of course your parents will be want to fly over as soon as they can… Alison's going to be beside herself with joy. You'll have to tell me what she says! I expect you'll want to phone her as soon as possible. It's wonderful, isn't it?'

CHAPTER NINE

'I'VE BEEN THINKING…' Georgina didn't look at Matias as she said that. She busied herself sweeping up the suit jacket he had discarded on the kitchen counter and the tie which he had dropped to the ground. The jacket would have cost what most people might earn in six months, and the tie was the softest of silk.

She had discovered that Matias treated his clothes with the casual disregard of someone who knew that he could snap his fingers and replace the lot at a moment's notice. However, it went against the grain for Georgina to accept this cavalier indifference to possessions that cost the earth.

'You've been thinking…?' Matias drawled, sitting on a kitchen chair and swivelling it so that he could stretch his long legs out in front of him.

Summer had abruptly turned into a rainy, bleak autumn, and outside the relentlessly blue skies had become a thing of the past. Now, a fine, persistent drizzle was drumming against the window panes. Nothing like the savage downpour that had accompanied that very first time they had made love, but weedy and insistent and never-ending.

Something smelled good. Georgina not only photographed food but had also proved herself to be more than competent when faced with cooking it.

'You're doing an awful lot of travelling to and from here.' She leaned against the counter and looked at him with clear, level green eyes. 'I've had a lot of interest after my last shoot—from people in London and a publishing house in France, of all places. I feel that it might further my career if I moved to London.'

She could have added that the frequency of his visits to Cornwall was no longer strictly necessary. It was over a month since Rose had had her operation, and she was now back on her feet and wondering why on earth Georgina wasn't thinking about moving to London.

'After all,' Rose had pointed out, 'it's not as though Matias is ever going to contemplate moving down here full time, and commuting can't be a long-term proposition. I'm back to rights, and if I'm going to be moving into something smaller in the village I shall feel quite capable of being on my own. You two need to think about what's going to work for you…'

Georgina thought uneasily about the engagement that had only been put in place as a temporary measure. She'd held off telling her parents, because she knew that involving more people than strictly necessary—especially her parents—would be to start hurtling down a dangerous slope, but the fact of the matter was that she and Matias were lovers, and still no mention had been made of timelines.

That being the case, this didn't seem too dramatic a step forward. Did it…?

'Is my mother behind this sudden decision?'

Something in his voice made the hairs on the back of her neck stand on end, and something in those cool dark eyes was setting alarm bells ringing in her head. However, having put one foot on this road, she now felt obliged to carry on.

'She *has* been wondering why you're continuing to commute. I know you spend a couple of days a week down here, but the rest of the time you're up and down, and she thinks it's weird for a newly engaged couple not to be trying to find a solution so that they can be together a bit more.'

'Is that a fact…?'

Matias stood up and strolled to the window to stare silently outside for a few seconds before turning back to look at her. His expression was shuttered, unreadable.

'I wouldn't normally consider moving as an option but, like I said, I've had a lot of interest from two companies in London and one in France. The Paris one is obviously… You know… Actually, they want to set up a meeting with me…'

She knew that she was stammering and her voice tapered off into a lengthening silence as he continued to look at her for a while without saying anything.

Georgina recalled the knotted stomach she had had when she had first gone to his house to tell him of her hare-brained idea to rescue his mother from her downward spiral of depression.

The knotted stomach was there again.

'It's not what you want to hear?' she said flatly.

Matias inclined his head to one side. 'No,' he returned. 'It's not.'

'Why not?' Georgina asked bluntly.

'The fact is, I've been doing some thinking of my own.'

He glanced across to where a pot was simmering on the stove, to the bottle of wine on the kitchen table, to the jacket and tie which had been neatly tidied away—all trappings of a domesticity he had always shunned.

'My mother is back on her feet. The operation was a success, as I knew it would be. She's now strong enough, in my opinion, to deal with the fact that there isn't going to be any walk down the aisle.'

His fabulous eyes were the colour of wintry seas and his expression was remote—the expression of someone retreating and walking away.

'Of *course* there's not going to be a walk down the aisle.' She felt sick, dizzy, and she was sure that it showed on her face because she could feel her colour draining away. 'That's not what this suggestion is about. Yes, it makes sense if this engagement is going to continue, but also I really have a chance of developing my career if I move out of Cornwall.'

'This is my fault,' Matias breathed with self-condemnation.

'I have no idea what you're talking about.'

'Don't you, Georgie?'

'No. I don't.' She kept her voice cool. 'And I wish I'd never said anything.'

'Look around,' Matias told her quietly. 'You're cooking for me…you're tidying up behind me… Somewhere along the line you've started the business of trying to domesticate me.'

'Matias, I'm doing no such thing! And please don't forget that it was *your* idea to take things one step further by pretending to be engaged! And if I'm cooking, and tidying up your clothes, have you stopped to think that it's because you happen to be staying in *my* house and I don't want to see clothes everywhere? And I have to cook for myself so I might as well cook for you as well.'

She tilted her chin at a defiant angle, and in return Matias looked back at her with appreciation.

'I'm not up for grabs, Georgie. And the reason I blame myself is because you were wet behind the ears and a virgin. I should have known that there was always going to be a danger that you might start confusing fantasy with reality…start thinking about a relationship I'd never have time for. I wanted you—and I took what I wanted because I'm a selfish bastard.'

Georgina's eyes flashed and she held his stare steadily. 'Don't try and take responsibility for this,

Matias, and please don't try and make out that I want all this to be real. I might be inexperienced, but I'm not an imbecile. I didn't have to carry on sleeping with you after that first night. If you took what you wanted, then has it occurred to you that I did the same? Took what *I* wanted?'

'Is that your story and you're sticking to it?'

'I *haven't* started confusing reality with fantasy,' she said through gritted teeth.

And she hadn't. She knew that their engagement was a sham, but the truth was that she'd begun to hope… They'd slipped into a comfortable zone, and she'd started hoping that beneath that comfort there was something substantial for him, just as it had become substantial for her. She'd deluded herself into thinking that the sizzling sex and their easy familiarity amounted to more than it obviously did.

He hadn't been lulled into wanting her more because of what they'd ended up sharing. He'd ended up having to deal with just the sort of unwelcome expectations that got on his nerves.

'Okay.'

He shot her a crooked smile, which made her teeth snap together in frustration because of the disbelief he couldn't be bothered to conceal. But she knew that it should come as no surprise. His history with women told its own story, and she had chosen to ignore all the warnings he had put out there at her own peril. He was too astute when it came to the opposite sex not to have noticed those sidelong glances, the tender touches and, yes, that slide into domesticity that said more than words ever could about what they had and what it signified for her.

If, however, he thought that she was going to break down and start getting emotional, then he had another think coming—because no way was she going to do that.

'Perfectly understandable to call off the engagement at this stage,' she informed him. 'You're right. Rose is in a much better place now that the operation is out of the way and she's been given a clean bill of health. Also it suits me, because I can focus exclusively on seeing where my career takes me now that my field is expanding.'

'So you do intend to move to London?'

'Possibly. I don't know.' She fiddled with the ring on her finger, then removed it and slid it over to him. 'I don't want this. The thought of keeping something "for services rendered" makes me feel sick.'

'Georgie...' Matias stared at the ring but didn't pick it up. Instead he raised his eyes to hers and held her gaze. 'This is for the best.'

'I know,' she said sweetly. 'I think I've already heard that speech from you. Remember? When you were getting rid of the Amazonian blonde?'

'This is hardly the same sort of situation.'

Georgina shrugged. 'It is—more or less. It's a break-up...one that was always expected. But there's no need for you to spin the line about you being bad for me.'

'It wouldn't be a lie.'

'Nor would it be relevant.' She looked at him defiantly, challenging him to take her up on that statement. When he didn't, she continued, 'I'll talk to Rose…let her down gently.'

'You can leave that to me,' Matias muttered heavily. 'Like I said—and whether you choose to believe me or not—I blame myself…'

'If you want to be a martyr then I can't stop you. But I'm not blaming you, so there's no need for you to jump in and throw yourself in front of the train. At any rate you're no longer the bad guy in the story. You've built a great relationship with your mother. Don't jeopardise that by being the one to let her down. I don't want her assuming that you're leaving a heartbroken wreck behind because you couldn't resist returning to your revolving door love life.' She tilted her head at an angle, eyes cool.

'What will you say?' Matias asked, recognising the stubborn set of her jaw.

'That things didn't work out in the end but that we're going to remain good friends.'

She stood up and wondered how the rest of the evening was going to play out after this conversation. She couldn't see some cosy chat over the chicken casserole followed by a romp in the sack. What she *could* see was her howling to the four winds because the void opening up in front of her made her feel nauseous and lost and defeated.

'I'll leave now.'

Matias had read her mind and stood up. He hesitated and Georgina spoke quickly, before pity could cloud his face and before he could reopen the conversation about it all being his fault.

'Good idea. I think that's for the best. Will you take all your stuff? Or I'm quite happy to drop it off to your mum's house.'

'Are you going to be okay?'

'Just go, Matias. The last thing I need is for you to tell me how sorry you feel for me. I always saw this coming and I'm absolutely fine.'

Still he hesitated, before finally turning round and leaving the kitchen—leaving her standing there on her own, unable to move a muscle.

She heard the sound of his footsteps receding, then eventually the sound of him coming down the stairs. She heard him pause and she knew that he was debating whether he should come over…say goodbye… make sure she hadn't stuck her head in the oven. Because she was obviously so pathetic that not only had she fallen for him but now—now that the rug had been pulled from underneath her fragile little feet—she would end up going to pieces and falling apart at the seams unless he produced some bracing words of encouragement.

Okay, so perhaps she *was* going to fall apart at the seams, and perhaps she *would* go to pieces, but she would do it in her own time and then she would start rebuilding her life. Away from Cornwall…away from the memories.

* * *

Matias stared moodily out of the window of his plush office on the thirtieth floor of a towering glass building which represented the very summit of what his vast reserves of wealth could achieve. Only the privileged few could afford to breathe the rarefied atmosphere up here.

Someone was saying something, and he registered that it involved making yet more money with yet another deal of even more magnitude than the last one.

Ten days.

Ten days since everything had crashed and burned, leaving behind a restlessness that got on his nerves. He'd always had complete control over his life, but for the first time he was floundering, and it was a sensation that was driving him crazy.

He'd spoken to his mother but hadn't enquired after Georgina's whereabouts. Several times he had begun to dial her number but had terminated the call before it could connect.

True to her word, she had told his mother exactly what she had said she would. His mother, predictably, had been bitterly disappointed, but she had dealt with the disappointment and had reached out to him to console him.

It was only now that he had engaged with her that he realised exactly how much distance he had allowed to settle between them. He had allowed his childhood experiences to dictate the outcome of his relationship with his parents and that had been a mistake. The fact that things were settling into a different place now had given his mother a renewed lease of life.

'If you two found that you couldn't make it work,' she had said sadly, when he had phoned her the day after Georgina had disappeared, 'then it's for the best that you called it a day before you took the next step forward and found yourself married. So much more difficult to unravel a relationship at that point.'

'We did our utmost to make it work, but I'm not the easiest person in the world to…er…to…'

His mother had interrupted him to assure him firmly that no blame had been put on his shoulders. Since then, even though he had spoken to his mother every day, she had said nothing whatsoever about Georgina and pride had prevented Matias from asking.

She'd made her decision, he thought, and she would get on with her life. She was better off without him, anyway, whether she chose to believe that or not. And he'd had a narrow escape. He'd recognised the signs of her falling for him. She might not have admitted it, but he wasn't blind. Yes, far better that they'd parted company—and if she was still on his mind, it was because he was worried about her.

He was interrupted mid-thought by someone addressing him directly, and he turned round, frowning.

Six people were sitting around the glass and chrome conference table in his office, but for the first time in his high-powered, meteoric career Matias was finding it difficult to focus. With the decisiveness so typical of his forceful, aggressive personality, he told them, without preamble, that the meeting was over.

'My PA will be in touch tomorrow and my CEO Harper will carry on with proceedings from here on in.'

He was feeling better already—because he was doing something…taking charge of this vaguely uncomfortable situation that had been distracting him since she'd gone. He was sick to death of *thinking*.

He watched as everyone began gathering up their belongings after a brief moment of utter confusion. He waited. Not moving. Waited until they had all cleared out of his office then he got his mother on the phone.

Second by second, his mood was lifting.

'Where is she?' he asked, as soon as his mother had answered the phone.

'Darling, it's very nice to hear your voice,' Rose answered with some surprise. 'Would you be talking about Georgie?'

'You know I am, and tell me you're not avoiding my question…' he countered drily, settling into his leather chair and swivelling it so that he was staring out of the window to an uninterrupted view of milky blue sky.

'I feel that if Georgina wanted to get in touch with you then perhaps she would have,' Rose pointed out pragmatically.

'Granted. But…'

'But?'

He cleared his throat. 'I feel we still have some talking to do.'

'After all this time?'

'Ten days. That's not long. I… What is she up to? I… You know what I'm like… I want to make sure that she's…okay. Naturally I would phone myself, but if she wants some time out…' His voice tapered off.

'That's thoughtful of you, and you'll be pleased to hear that she's doing well, Matias. At least, that's what she said when I spoke to her the day before yesterday.'

There was another brief moment's hesitation, during which Matias jumped in, his voice irritable. 'Good! Glad to hear that she's doing well. Excellent!'

'She was very excited before she went,' Rose mused, 'but I could detect a certain nervousness underneath the excitement. Understandable, of course…'

'Went? Went where?' His senses were suddenly on red alert, his brain whirring round and round as he tried to compute what that throwaway remark meant.

'Did she not tell you? No, of course she wouldn't have, if you two haven't been in touch. Such a shame… I would have mentioned it to you, but, as I said, I felt that Georgina would tell you herself if she wanted you to know. Maybe she got the impression that you might not be interested?'

'Mother, where did she go?' Matias paused. Then, 'I just want to make sure that everything's all right with her.'

'Because you usually leave a string of broken hearts behind you, Matias? Not in this case. Georgina made it absolutely clear that *she* was the one with the second thoughts.'

Matias couldn't prevent an appreciative smile. He could just imagine the conversation. 'Where is she? If she's okay, then maybe I'm the one who isn't.' Something punched him in the gut, shaking his foundations.

'Oh, Georgina's taken a wonderful job,' Rose confided. 'She was offered it quite out of the blue... I think she was under the impression that most of the work would be done over here, but it turned out that they were so impressed with what they saw they invited her to go to Paris for a six-month secondment to work on a fabulous new magazine that's about to hit the streets there. Provincial French cooking. She's been asked to be the lead photographer. Such a great opportunity.'

'Paris? *Paris?*'

'I was a bit concerned as well, darling. You know our Georgie hasn't travelled far and wide. But she introduced me to the lovely guy she'll be working with...'

'Lovely guy?'

'Jacques something-or-other. Looks a little unconventional, but absolutely charming.'

'Jacques something-or-other...?' Matias gritted.

'Are you feeling all right?' Rose asked.

'Never been better. Sit tight, Mother. I'm heading down to Cornwall. I'll be there in a few hours.'

He didn't give his mother any time to question the decision. He knew what he had to do and he knew why he had to do it.

Paris?

Jacques something-or-other?

Georgina was in a fragile place. He had turned her away, just as he had turned away every other woman who had dared venture into the forbidden territory of wanting more than he was programmed to give. He'd been too abrupt—had overlooked the fact that she *wasn't* like all those other hard-nosed women he had dated in the past. She wasn't equipped to get past a broken relationship just by hitting the clubbing scene.

She'd been defiant and stood her ground, had denied every insinuation from him that she'd broken the rules of the game and fallen for him, but she had and she would be vulnerable. Vulnerable and in Paris. And that was a very bad combination, because vulnerable women had a way of appealing to just the kind of men they didn't need.

Who the hell was this Jacques character anyway?

He needed to find out exactly where she was! And if she needed to be rescued then, by God, he wasn't going to shy away from the task.

At last he was doing something. And he hadn't felt this good in a while.

It was after ten by the time Georgina stepped out of the taxi. The past week had been a frenetic round of social events, because everyone at the smart Parisian publishing house had wanted to make her feel at home and she couldn't have been more grateful.

She'd really needed this job—had yearned for the distraction it offered. She'd agreed to every term and condition and had been eloquent in persuading them that the sooner she was on board, the better. No sooner had the ink dried on the contract she had signed than she had been in Paris, ready to fling herself head-first into the commission—anything to lessen the pain of no longer having Matias in her life.

Accommodation had been found fast and everyone had gone out of their way to welcome her.

Tonight she had been for a casual meal in a lively bar with three of her colleagues and she was exhausted. Exhaustion was good, though, because the minute her mind stopped working in overdrive the thoughts began kicking in, and when that happened it was like spiralling down a bottomless hole.

Thoughts of Matias...of what it had been like with him and the way she had discovered that you didn't need to spend years finding out about someone to know that you loved them. It could happen in the snap of a finger. She thought about the way he had made her body sing, the things he would murmur when they made love. She hated it, but she was captive to the torment of remembering.

She was a million miles away when she became aware of someone stepping out of the shadows—a looming figure that sent her into a panic.

She didn't think. She acted completely on impulse. Because figures stepping out from the shadows were never going to be pleasant surprises.

She swung her handbag and she swung it hard. She aimed straight for the torso and she struck with perfect timing.

'Georgie!'

Georgina froze. She recognised that low, velvety voice instantly, but it still took her a couple of seconds to react, and then she sprang back and stared up, open-mouthed, as Matias straightened.

'Matias? *What are you doing here?*'

'I…' He shook his head and looked away briefly. 'I've come to talk to you,' he said in a low, driven undertone.

'Is that right? Well, I can't think of anything we have to talk about—and how did you get hold of my address? How did you even know where I was?'

'My mother told me.'

'She had no right.'

'She didn't think it was a state secret. Let me in, Georgie.' Matias paused. 'Please. Remember there was a time when you showed up at my house…did I refuse you entry?'

Georgina eyed him sourly. He was in black jeans and a black tee shirt and some kind of bomber jacket, and he looked utterly and unfairly drop-dead gorgeous.

'Time's moved on since then, wouldn't you say?' She was proud of how she sounded, which was a lot more controlled than she was feeling. 'One cup of coffee, Matias, and then I'm going to have to ask you to leave.'

They rode the elevator in silence, and she opened her front door and preceded him into the apartment without looking at him, although she was aware of his presence with every ounce of her perspiring body.

She dumped her handbag and the backpack holding her camera equipment on the granite counter separating the kitchen from the living room and faced Matias with her arms belligerently folded.

'Why are you here?'

'I had no idea that you'd taken yourself out of the country. Do you have anything to drink?'

Georgina gritted her teeth and glared. 'I have coffee. Like I said.'

'Anything stronger?'

'No.'

'I deserve this…' he muttered.

'You broke off an engagement that wasn't even an engagement.' Georgina shrugged. 'No big deal.'

'Why did you feel that you had to take a job over here?'

She flushed and her eyes skittered away. Her whole body was rigid with tension. Why had he come? She didn't want to *like* the fact that he was here, but she did. She didn't want her body to *feel* like this, hot and flustered and excited, but it did.

Would he ever stop having this sort of effect on her? she wondered despairingly. Would she bump into him in three years' time, when he had another woman hanging like a limpet off his arm, and feel this same surge of unwelcome attraction? Was that her fate?

'They made me an offer I couldn't refuse.' She lowered her eyes and started making a pot of coffee.

The apartment was purpose-built, in a new block, and the gadgets were all brand-new. It was very different from her parents' house, where everything harked back to days gone by, from the crockery to the appliances.

'I thought you were going to take something in London.'

'Does it matter? Is that why you rushed over here? Because you were concerned that I wouldn't be able to cope with a change of country?'

'You don't have much experience of big city living,' Matias muttered. 'You've lived in a small village all your life.'

'I can't believe I'm hearing this.' Georgina dumped the cup of coffee in front of him and then sprang back and glared at him. 'How incompetent do you think I am, Matias? First you thought that you had to run as fast as you could because I'd made the mistake of falling for you! Did you think that I was daydreaming about actually marrying you and living happily ever after? With a guy who's made a career out of making sure he doesn't get too involved with a woman? Oh, yes, of *course* you did! I mention that I might find it helpful to move to London to progress my career and all of a sudden I've turned into a starry-eyed idiot who wants to settle down with you for real!'

She heard the ring of outrage in her voice and felt the sting of pain in her heart. She'd started deluding herself into thinking about happy-ever-afters. She'd been a fool and he'd run away for a very good reason. She would never admit what she felt for him to his face, but it was something she would never be able to hide from herself, and denying her love, as she was doing now, was an agonising reminder of the truth.

'It's possible you may have got that impression,' Matias muttered, not giving an inch, programmed to defend his choices, whatever the provocation.

'And second—' Georgina had to stop herself from yelling as she overrode his interruption '—to add insult to injury, you storm over here on a mission, I presume, to save me from myself!'

'Did I say that?'

'Pretty much, Matias! I'm a simpleton from Cornwall, who's so accustomed to village life that I couldn't possibly handle the trauma of big city living!'

'You're putting words into my mouth,' he said, but he was uncomfortably aware that that was precisely the impression he had given when he had shown up unannounced. The time had come to set the record straight. But setting records straight had never felt so momentous an uphill climb, and he was so far out of his comfort zone that he could scarcely corral his thoughts.

'I'm doing no such thing, Matias Silva!' She glared. 'That's *exactly* what you said! Did you think that I would find it all too much, living over here? In Paris? Well, for your information, I'm absolutely *loving* it over here!'

'Are you?'

'Yes! The job is invigorating! I'm learning all sorts of new camera techniques! I'm working alongside a talented crew of people and it's fabulous being in a corporate atmosphere instead of doing my own thing!'

'So you don't miss anything about…anything at all…?' Matias inserted roughly.

She tilted her chin at a challenging angle. The thought of him feeling sorry for her was unbearable. Had Rose somehow implied that she was having a miserable time over here? She had made sure to sound as chirpy as a cricket in all her conversations with the older woman! But had Rose heard the unhappiness in her tone of voice and mistakenly assumed it was down to the job rather than down to the fact that her heart had been broken in two?

'Nothing,' she asserted firmly. 'Nothing at all.'

CHAPTER TEN

MATIAS HESITATED. HE wondered if this was what it felt like to have one foot dangling over the edge of a precipice, with no safety net below. He'd become accustomed to exercising complete control over every aspect of his life, so this was a first, sitting here, staring at the woman who had been in his head ever since he had walked away from her, knowing what he had to do and what he had to say and yet fearful of an outcome he couldn't predict.

'I didn't come here because I thought you couldn't cope…with…with life in a big city…'

'That's not what you said.'

'And it's what I told myself when I decided to fly over,' Matias admitted unevenly.

Restless, he sprang to his feet, lean body taut with suppressed tension, and paced the small kitchen before sinking back into the chair. but this time leaning forward towards her, elbows on thighs.

'I told myself that I was worried about you…that it was a perfectly understandable reaction. But that's not why I came, Georgie.'

'Good.'

Something about the uncertain expression on his face was striking a chord inside her, eroding her determination to stand her ground proudly and get rid of him as fast as she could. Since when did Matias Silva ever look uncertain?

'I had to come. I had to talk to you.'

Georgina folded her arms and didn't say anything. Silence, he had once told her, was always a successful ploy when it came to getting other people to say things they might not have banked on saying. What better time to try it out for herself?

'I've been…thinking about you, Georgie… I haven't been able to focus…'

Georgina stiffened. He was a man who was only about sex—it didn't take a genius to figure out why she'd been on his mind. It would certainly explain the hesitancy on his face.

'In that case,' she told him coldly, 'you've had a wasted trip.'

'What do you mean?' He looked at her narrowly, but the ground was slowly giving way under his feet and he couldn't think straight.

'I *mean*,' she said quietly, as the energy for a fight seeped out of her, 'I'm not returning to any sort of relationship with you.'

'You're not?'

'Matias…' She tugged her fingers through her long, unruly hair and sat facing him, chin propped in her hand, green eyes sad and pensive. 'I know what this is about. You tell me that I've been on your mind...that you can't focus? I realise that what you want to say is that you miss the sex. But I won't be coming back to you to pick up where we left off until you get genuinely bored with me. We had a clean break and now I'm moving forward.'

'You can't be.'

Georgina laughed shortly. *How dared he?* 'Really, Matias? And why's that?'

'Maybe because *I'm* not, and I'm desperate enough to hope that I'm not alone in that.'

His voice was a mumble and she had to strain to pick up what he had said.

'I don't know what you're trying to say, Matias,' she told him bluntly, just in case hope started sprouting shoots and staging a takeover.

'I haven't come here because I miss the sex. I haven't come here to rescue you from your decision to leave England. I've come here because I *haven't* moved on.'

He sat back, swept his hands through his hair, his eyes not quite meeting hers, and then he sighed and pressed his fingers against his eyes.

'I never realised it before and maybe I should have,' he muttered in a shaken voice, watching as she inclined her head to one side, wary and attentive at the same time.

'What do you mean? And please don't spin me any stories, Matias. Don't say stuff you don't mean because you think it'll make me feel better or worse, or because you think it might get me back into bed with you. *What* have you never realised before?'

'When you waltzed into my house you were the last person I expected. You'd never been to see me before. You'd never expressed any desire to come to London. You'd never shown any interest in what sort of life I led there, or what sort of place I lived in. And yet…'

'And yet…?'

'And yet I wasn't fazed. I didn't stop to think about that. I should have. If I had, I would have realised that you and I…we have so much history between us. I've known you for ever.'

'And that's a *good* thing?' Georgina asked gruffly. 'Matias, you've always struck me as someone who likes novelty. Even when we embarked on…on the physical side of things, I got the impression that I was…a novelty…a change from your usual type of woman…'

'I deserve that.' He met her gaze evenly and then shook his head with regret. 'My priorities were cemented when I was too young to question them. My parents lived from one day to the next. I hated that…'

His voice was halting as he began to explore emotional territory he had always been loath to cover. He raked his fingers through his hair and realised that they weren't quite as steady as he might have hoped. The weird thing, he thought, was that she *knew* all of this—either by inference or because he had told her in some way, shape or form during the time they had spent together. And yet tension was snaking through him, strangling his vocal cords and blurring his thoughts.

'I don't suppose they ever gave it a moment's thought, but their lifestyle made me realise that the one and only thing I wanted from life was security. Financial security. I'd watched as they bounced from one scheme to another. I stopped focusing on the fact that they were perfectly happy doing that. I stopped focusing on the fact that their choices didn't impede on their responsibility as parents. I only saw...'

Georgina reached out and impulsively rested her hand on his, barely registering that he didn't remove it, that he covered it with his own.

'I suppose,' Matias said pensively, 'that going to boarding school conferred innumerable advantages upon me, but there were also warnings there that I was too young to interpret. I was an impressionable adolescent, and my parents' hippy lifestyle suffered in contrast to the well-ordered lifestyles of the well-heeled kids I was suddenly having to live with. I didn't envy what they had, but bit by bit I knew, whatever their private lives might have been, that financial security was something that *protected* them—like varnish on wood. By the time I left that school my ambitions were in place. And there was no room in that agenda for relationships.'

'So you enjoyed women for a while and then... then you moved on...?'

'Something like that.' He smiled crookedly—a

heartbreaking smile that made her jaw tighten. 'But I'm straying off-topic here. I… I think I might need something stronger than coffee.'

'I have some red wine…' Georgina began, standing, but he wouldn't release her hand.

'Maybe not. Georgie, let's sit somewhere more comfortable.' He indicated the sofa in the sitting room of the open-plan apartment. 'Maybe I need to say what I need to say without the help of alcohol but not in an upright metal chair.'

'Am I going to like what I hear?'

'Depends on what you want to hear.'

'I'll withhold judgement until I've listened to what you have to say.'

But she knew that she was losing perspective. He was so…so much a piece of her…so spellbinding… just so beautiful… And right now he was as open as she had ever seen him, and that, in itself, riveted her attention and made her heart beat so fast that she wanted to pass out.

'When you walked through the door of my house that very first time it felt natural. I guess I should start with that. Though it was something that hardly registered with me then. Your scheme was crazy. It was also the most generous thing anyone could have done. Generous and impulsive. I turned you away because I was accustomed to being the one in control, and then, when I did decide to go along with your charade…'

'Your first idea was to get me to dress the part.'

Georgina gave him a tentative smile. She had given up trying to work out where this was leading. It was honest, and that was the main thing. She would deal with wherever it ended up when it got there.

'I couldn't resist you,' Matias said simply. 'Somewhere along the line, on some level I didn't consciously understand, I accepted that a change of wardrobe had nothing to do with the level of sexual pull you had over me. I don't think there was a single minute I didn't look at you without wanting to touch you. You have no idea what a big deal it was for me to make love to you that first time… You trusted me enough to gift me with your virginity and that wasn't just a big deal to you. It was a big deal to me too, even if I didn't appreciate just how big at the time. Didn't appreciate,' he tacked on roughly, 'just how privileged I was.'

Georgina tensed, reluctant to talk about it. She didn't want her emotional vulnerability paraded. She looked around her at the trappings of independence. *This* was the woman she was now, she told herself. She couldn't afford to succumb to the temptation of what he was saying.

'But you still got scared when I mentioned that I might want to see what London held for me,' she reminded him tautly.

'I reacted predictably.' Matias was honest. 'Everything seemed to coalesce in my head all at once. The fake engagement…the trappings of domesticity that had somehow taken over, bit by bit…the situation that suddenly felt like the sort of slippery slope downwards I had always avoided.'

Hot colour stung her cheeks. 'I never meant to try and trap you,' she said stiffly.

'But you had anyway.'

'How so, Matias…?'

She was determined not to wear her heart on her sleeve—not for a second time—but she knew that her voice was betraying that good intention.

'Somehow I'd managed to drift into a pattern of behaviour…commuting to and from London, coming down to Cornwall, taking my jacket off and slinging somewhere, accepting that you would do what you always did and pick it up, hang it up. And…'

He gave her a crooked smile.

'And tell me that I had more money than sense. I'm not sure when I started to accept that level of easy, cosy familiarity without automatically railing against it. I just know that something sparked inside me. Maybe it was the way I noticed you looking at that engagement ring, as though it was the real thing… Maybe it was when it struck me that I *liked* it—that I *liked* returning to your side, looked *forward* to seeing you…touching you…holding you…*talking* to you… But suddenly… I don't know…the shutters slammed down. Old habits die hard. I'd become so accustomed to assuming that love was something other people did that I reacted instinctively. I had to break off the engagement, had to escape, and I told myself that it was for the best.'

'You looked forward to seeing me? Talking to me?'

'You'd managed to tame me, and I couldn't even work out when it had happened. I just knew that it scared the living daylights out of me, and the only way I could cope with that realisation was to run away from it as fast as I could.'

'I never knew…' she murmured softly.

Her heart was pounding, her pulses were racing and the time for games was over. He'd said so much, and now it was her turn to go the final mile and say what was in her heart.

'Why would you? I barely knew myself,' he said.

'I…' She took a deep breath. 'I never, *ever* thought we would end up in bed together. When we did, it felt so good, Matias, so *right*. Only afterwards, when the dust had settled, it slowly dawned on me that the reason it felt so good—the reason I hadn't had a moment's doubt about losing my virginity to you—was because I *loved* you.'

He moved to speak.

'Please don't say anything. Please let me get this off my chest and finish saying what I have to say. You've come this far to say your piece. Well, I might as well return the favour. Being engaged to you, even though I *knew* that it wasn't a real engagement, felt like a dream come true. I didn't like it that it did, but I couldn't pretend otherwise. And then, somewhere along the line, I started thinking that we got along so well… I fantasised that you might realise that it was more than just the fact that we got along between the sheets. But the weird thing was that even though I *knew* it was all going to end in heartbreak for me, I never regretted a single second of what we had.'

'And now here we are again.'

'I can't believe you've come all the way over here, but I'm glad you have.' *Glad that I've put my heart on the line, whatever the outcome.* It felt as if a weight had been lifted from her shoulders.

'I had to. I'm in love with you.'

Georgina had spun so many daydreams about Matias uttering those very words, and in all those daydreams she had squealed with delight and clapped her hands and smothered him in kisses. But actually, now that he had spoken them, what she felt was a spreading warmth, as though a candle had been lit inside her.

He pulled her towards him, manoeuvred her so that she was sitting on his lap and kissed her—a soft, tender kiss that melted everything inside her…a kiss she never wanted to end.

When, eventually, he drew back from her, she wished that she could bottle the loving expression in his eyes.

'So will you marry me, Georgie?'

'Do you even have to ask? Surely you must know the answer to that? Just try and stop me, Matias Silva.' She linked her fingers behind his neck and smiled. 'Don't forget you've already bought me the engagement ring of my dreams…'

* * *

Georgina heard the sound of Matias's car on the gravel outside and her heart leapt, as it always did at the sound of his arrival.

She looked around, making sure everything was just right. Dimmed lights. Candles on the table. The smell of wonderful food.

She had followed three of the fantastic recipes from the French cookery magazine on which she had worked. It had felt strange to look at the photos she had taken and attach them to the recipes she'd so diligently followed.

Her stint in Paris felt like a lifetime ago, but then, as she'd reflected on more than one occasion, it would, wouldn't it? Because so much had happened since then.

On that dreamy morning after the night when every single wish she'd ever had and a million more she hadn't even been aware of having had all come true, she'd woken up with Matias next to her in bed. In her wonderful apartment in Paris.

'I've been thinking,' he'd drawled, pulling her against him so that their warm, newly awoken bodies were pressed against each other. 'You should stay here and finish what you've started. I have an office in Paris and, coincidentally, I also have an apartment. We could have some fun here together before we return to London.'

They'd had a lot of fun. Her six-month secondment had been absolute bliss. She'd debated whether to remain in her own apartment, but in the end it had seemed silly because she'd spent so much of her time with Matias—who, in fairness, hadn't objected when she'd wanted to go out with work colleagues on her own, and had always been willing to accompany her if she asked.

They'd returned to London and the preparations for their big day had begun in earnest, with Rose having a lot of input—more than Georgie's own mother, who had descended in a flurry of excitement only a month before the big day.

Which, as it happened, had been just the right size sort of day. Friends, family, a handful of her work colleagues—including some of the people she had met in Paris, with whom she was determined to stay in contact. And some of Matias's colleagues as well—a couple of whom had privately confessed to her that they'd never thought they'd see the day.

Nor had he, she'd wanted to say.

They were married in the local church in Cornwall, and then he'd whisked her away to the Maldives for their honeymoon.

It was the first real holiday he had ever had as an adult. Which was just one of those incidental admissions that made her see how much he trusted her by confiding in her.

And as soon as they'd returned the big decision had begun as to where they would live.

Not Cornwall, and Georgina was happy with that—especially after her stint in Paris, where she had tasted life in a big city, and not just in the capacity of tourist. She had made numerous connections while she had been out there.

She'd told Matias she was happy to acquiesce to life in his London house, which was big enough to house a small battalion. But Matias had looked at her thoughtfully and suggested that perhaps London wasn't quite the place for them.

'At least, not central London,' he had mused. 'I think I've become accustomed quite quickly to having peaceful downtime with you. Without the sound of traffic outside my front window.'

'You hardly live on a busy street over a parade of shops, Matias,' Georgina had pointed out wryly, which had made him burst out laughing.

In the end they had decided to move out towards Richmond. Close enough to the city for Matias to commute—although he was fast discovering the joys of flexible working hours which, as the guy who ran the whole show, he could take at the click of a finger.

The house was enormous by London standards, with a sprawling garden, and the entire transaction had been completed in record time. Money talked.

Now they had been living here for a little over four months and...

Georgina looked around her. Looked at the beautiful kitchen table, the impeccable worktops, the flagstone tiles on the floor which they had chosen together.

Every single little thing had been hand-picked.

Having lived under her parents' roof while they were on the other side of the world, Georgina had been able to bring precious little to the table, so Matias had insisted on starting from scratch.

She looked up to see the man of her dreams standing in the doorway. He had shed his coat and was rolling up the sleeves of his white shirt, but he paused, eyebrows raised, taking in the table-setting.

'Tell me I haven't missed an important anniversary,' he drawled, smiling and pulling her towards him so that he could kiss her—a long, lingering, loving kiss.

Georgina breathed in his unique, woody smell, clean and musky at the same time, and as powerful an aphrodisiac as anyone could ever dream up. She wound her hands round his body and slipped her fingers under the waistband of his trousers.

'Nope...' she breathed a little unsteadily. 'My birthday isn't for another few weeks and there's no anniversary yet.'

'In that case...?'

He nodded to the elaborate setting and she smiled and tugged him into the kitchen, fingers linked, where she poured him a glass of wine while he peered into the oven, sniffing the aroma appreciatively.

'I just wanted the right mood board to tell you what I have to tell you.'

'Which is...?' He held her at arm's length and looked her directly in the eye.

'When I showed up on your doorstep and informed you that you were going to be my loving boyfriend,' she said seriously, which made his eyebrows shoot up with rampant amusement, 'I never thought that a year later I would be wearing your ring on my finger and I'd have gone from pretend loved-up girlfriend to wife for real...'

'Tell me about it... One minute I was dispatching a blonde because watching paint dry was turning out to be more fun than being with her, and the next minute my life was being turned upside down by a girl who'd been holding me to account from the day she'd learned to speak her first word...'

Georgina grinned, then stepped towards him and stroked the side of his cheek with the back of her hand. '*Someone* had to hold you to account, Matias Silva. But now that we're happily married it seems a little selfish to keep you all to myself, so I've decided to share you.'

'With...?'

'Gender to be decided. I should tell you that for the first couple of years conversation might be a little limited, but I can guarantee that you'll be in love with him. Or her.'

She patted her still flat stomach gently and then smiled when she saw his reaction, because it was everything she could have hoped for and more.

'My darling...' Matias breathed huskily. 'I love you so much.' He covered her hand with his. 'I don't know how I ever survived before you stormed into my life and took charge, even if you didn't know you were doing it...'

He grinned and nuzzled the side of her neck, and when their eyes met his were so full of love that the breath hitched in her throat and her eyes welled up— which was crazy.

'I'm going to be the best husband it's possible to be, Georgie, and the best father. And now...' He looked over her shoulder to the impeccably laid table. 'I think the food can wait for a bit, because I can think of a few more inventive ways for us to celebrate...'

* * * * *

If you enjoyed
Marriage Bargain with His Innocent
you're sure to enjoy these other stories
by Cathy Williams!

A Diamond Deal with Her Boss
The Italian's One-Night Consequence
The Tycoon's Ultimate Conquest
Contracted for the Spaniard's Heir

Available now!

Available May 21, 2019

#3721 THE SHEIKH CROWNS HIS VIRGIN
Billionaires at the Altar
by Lynne Graham
When Zoe is kidnapped, she's saved by Raj—an exiled desert prince. The attraction between them is instant! Yet her rescue comes with a price: to avoid a scandal, Zoe *must* become Raj's virgin bride...

#3722 SHOCK HEIR FOR THE KING
Secret Heirs of Billionaires
by Clare Connelly
Frankie is shocked when Matt, the stranger she gave her innocence to, reappears. Now she's in for the biggest shock of all—he's actually *King* Matthias! And to claim his heir, he demands Frankie become his queen!

#3723 GREEK'S BABY OF REDEMPTION
One Night With Consequences
by Kate Hewitt
When brooding billionaire Alex needs a wife to secure his business, his housekeeper, Milly, agrees. But their wedding night sparks an unexpected fire... Could Milly—and his unborn child—be the key to Alex's redemption?

#3724 UNTOUCHED UNTIL HER ULTRA-RICH HUSBAND
by Dani Collins
To avoid destitution, Luli needs outrageously wealthy Gabriel's help. The multi-billionaire's solution? He'll secure both their futures by marrying her! But after sweeping Luli into his luxurious world, Gabriel discovers the chemistry with his untouched wife is *priceless*...

#3725 A SCANDALOUS MIDNIGHT IN MADRID
Passion in Paradise
by Susan Stephens

A moonlit encounter tempts Sadie all the way to Alejandro's castle...and into his bed! But their night of illicit pleasure soon turns Sadie into Spain's most scandalous headline: *Pregnant with Alejandro's baby!*

#3726 UNTAMED BILLIONAIRE'S INNOCENT BRIDE
Conveniently Wed!
by Caitlin Crews

To prevent a scandal, Lauren needs to find reclusive Dominik—her boss's estranged brother—and convince him to marry her! As Dominik awakens her long-dormant desire, will Lauren accept that their hunger can't be denied?

#3727 CLAIMING HIS REPLACEMENT QUEEN
Monteverre Marriages
by Amanda Cinelli

Khalil's motivation for marriage is politics, not passion. Yet a sizzling encounter with his soon-to-be queen, Cressida, changes everything. And the desire innocent Cressida ignites is too hot to resist...

#3728 REUNITED BY THE GREEK'S VOWS
by Andie Brock

Kate is stunned when ex-fiancé, Nikos, storms back into her life—and demands they marry! Desperate to save her company, she agrees. But what these heated adversaries don't anticipate is that their still-smoldering flame will explode into irresistible passion...

---

*To avoid destitution, Luli needs outrageously wealthy
Gabriel's help. The multibillionaire's solution? He'll
secure both their futures by marrying her! But sweeping
Luli into his luxurious world, Gabriel discovers the
chemistry with his untouched wife is* priceless...

*Read on for a sneak preview of
Dani Collins's next story,*
Untouched Until Her Ultra-Rich Husband*!*

You told me what you were worth, Luli. Act like you believe it.

She had been acting. The whole time. Still was, especially as a handful
of designers whose names she knew from Mae's glossy magazines behaved
with deference as they welcomed her to a private showroom complete with
catwalk.

She had to fight back laughing with incredulity as they offered her
champagne, caviar, even a pedicure.

"I—" She glanced at Gabriel, expecting him to tell them she aspired to
model and should be treated like a clotheshorse, not royalty.

"A full wardrobe," he said. "Top to bottom, morning to night, office to
evening. Do what you can overnight, then send the rest to my address in
New York."

"Mais bien sûr, monsieur," the couturier said without a hint of falter in
her smile. "Our pleasure."

"Gabriel—" Luli started to protest as the women scattered.

"You remember what I said about this?" He tapped the wallet that held
her phone. "I need you to stay on brand."

"Reflect who you are?"

"Yes."

"Who are you?" she asked ruefully. "I only met you ten minutes ago."

"I'm a man who doesn't settle for anything less than the best." He
touched her chin. "The world is going to have a lot of questions about why
we married. Give them an answer."

His words roused the competitor who still lurked inside her. She wanted to prove to the world she was worthy to be his wife. Maybe she wanted to prove her worth to him, too. Definitely she longed to prove something to herself.

Either way, she made sure those long-ago years of preparation paid off. She had always been ruthless in evaluating her own shortcomings and knew how to play to her strengths. She might not be trying to win a crown today, but she hadn't been then, either. She'd been trying to win the approval of a woman who hadn't deserved her idolatry.

She pushed aside those dark memories and clung instead to the education she had gained in those difficult years.

"That neckline will make my shoulders look narrow," she said, making quick up-and-down choices. "The sweetheart style is better, but no ruffles at my hips. Don't show me yellow. Tangerine is better. A more verdant green. That one is too pale." In her head, she was sectioning out the building blocks of a cohesive stage presence. Youthful, but not too trendy. Sensual, but not overtly sexual. Charismatic without being showy.

"Something tells me I'm not needed," Gabriel said twenty minutes in and rose to leave. "We'll go for dinner in three hours." He glanced to the couturier. "And return in the morning for another fitting."

"Parfait. Merci, monsieur." Her smile was calm, but the way people were bustling told Luli how big a deal this was. How big a deal Gabriel was.

The women took her measurements while showing her unfinished pieces that only needed hemming or minimal tailoring so she could take them immediately.

"You'll be up all night," Luli murmured to one of the seamstresses.

The young woman moved quickly, but not fast enough for her boss, who kept crying, *"Vite! Vite!"*

"I'm sorry to put you through this," Luli added.

"Pas de problème. Monsieur Dean is a treasured client. It's our honor to provide your trousseau." She clamped her teeth on a pin between words. "Do you know where he's taking you for dinner? We should choose that dress next, so I can work on the alterations while you have your hair and makeup done. It must be fabulous. The world will be watching."

She would be presented publicly as his wife, Luli realized with a hard thump in her heart.

Don't miss
Untouched Until Her Ultra-Rich Husband.
Available June 2019 wherever
Harlequin® Presents books and ebooks are sold.

www.Harlequin.com

HARLEQUIN

Presents.

Coming next month—
a seductive Spanish romance!

In *A Scandalous Midnight in Madrid* by Susan Stephens,
Sadie is shocked by the red-hot connection she feels when
she encounters the aristocratic Spanish billionaire.
But what's even more shocking, is when she discovers
that she's pregnant with his baby...

Dedicated chef Sadie's life is changed forever by an
intense moonlit encounter in Madrid with infamous
Alejandro de Alegon. The sizzling anticipation he sparks
tempts virgin Sadie all the way to his Spanish castle...and
into his bed! She's never known anything like the wild passion
Alejandro unleashes. But when Sadie discovers their night of
illicit pleasure had consequences, she becomes Spain's biggest
headline: scandalously pregnant with Alejandro's baby!

A Scandalous Midnight in Madrid

Passion in Paradise

Available June 2019

HPBPA0519

Love Harlequin romance?

DISCOVER.

Be the first to find out about promotions, news and exclusive content!

 Facebook.com/HarlequinBooks

 Twitter.com/HarlequinBooks

 Instagram.com/HarlequinBooks

 Pinterest.com/HarlequinBooks

ReaderService.com

EXPLORE.

Sign up for the Harlequin e-newsletter and download a free book from any series at **TryHarlequin.com.**

CONNECT.

Join our Harlequin community to share your thoughts and connect with other romance readers!
Facebook.com/groups/HarlequinConnection

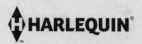

ROMANCE WHEN
YOU NEED IT

HSOCIAL2018

Want to give in to temptation with
steamy tales of irresistible desire?

Check out **Harlequin® Presents®,
Harlequin® Desire** and
Harlequin® Kimani™ Romance books!

New books available every month!

CONNECT WITH US AT:

Facebook.com/groups/HarlequinConnection

 Facebook.com/HarlequinBooks

 Twitter.com/HarlequinBooks

 Instagram.com/HarlequinBooks

 Pinterest.com/HarlequinBooks

ReaderService.com

**ROMANCE WHEN
YOU NEED IT**

PGENRE2018